Turn to Learn

30 Ready-to-Reproduce Wheels for Cross-Curricular Hands-on Learning

by Virginia Dooley

NEW YORK • TORONTO • LONDON • AUCKLAND • SYDNEY

Dedication

To my mother and father

Acknowledgments

Thanks to: Terry Cooper, Helen Sorvillo, and Carmen Sorvillo for all their help; Maria Fleming for her great ideas; James Graham Hale for his enthusiasm and wonderful art; and a special thanks to Louis Martino for his patience in getting many of these wheels to work.

Cover design by Vincent Ceci and Jaime Lucero
Cover illustrations by James Graham Hale
Interior design by Carmen Robert Sorvillo
Interior illustrations by James Graham Hale

ISBN 0-590-70134-7

12 11 10 9 8 7 6 5 4 3 2 7/9

Printed in the U.S.A.

Table of Contents

Introduction

The Wheels

Opposite Wheels

Thematic Wheels

Story Wheels

Math Wheels

Phonics Wheels

Blank Wheels

Introduction

Welcome to *Turn to Learn*! The 30 manipulative learning wheels in this book can be used in many ways in your classroom. Some of them, such as **Counting**, **Colors**, and **Clothes** are fun ways to introduce or reinforce basic concepts and vocabulary. Others, like **Humpty Dumpty** and **Jack and Jill** provide children with picture prompts for their own storytelling. And still others, such as **Bugs** and **Zoo Animals** are wonderful ways to add an exciting, hands-on activity to a thematic unit. Best of all, the wheels are fun to make and use, and provide you with another avenue for motivating your students.

How to Make the Wheels

Whenever possible, involve children in making the wheels themselves. Most of the wheels have been designed so that children can cut them out themselves using blunt-tipped scissors. The heavy solid lines are the cut lines; the dashed lines are fold lines.

Point out to children that there is a top and bottom wheel that need to be aligned. Children in second grade may be able to align the wheels and insert the paper fastener themselves. Kindergartners and first graders will need your help with this.

It will be easier for children to color the wheels before they attach them with the paper fastener. However, the two colors wheels (pages 20 and 22) work best as a teaching tool if they are colored after they are attached. Once they're constructed, children can color in the sections of the wheel to match the color word.

Some of the wheels are meant to be written on. The counting and number facts wheels, for example, include answer lines. Children can count or add the objects in the "window" and write in the number.

Supplies

To make these wheels your students will need paper, crayons or markers, scissors, and paper fasteners. If you decide to make sturdier wheels, you'll need tag board or you can use recycled manila folders. And if you decide to laminate them, you'll, of course, need a laminating machine.

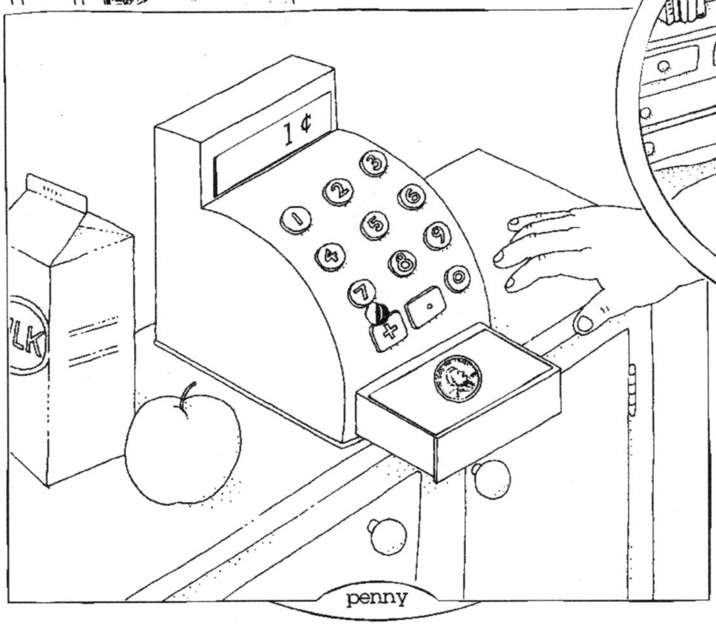

1¢

penny

A few of the wheels are more complicated, and you should either make some of the cuts yourself or get another adult to help you. Many teachers invite parent volunteers into the classroom to help, or send the wheels home. See the note about cutting below.

A Note About Cutting

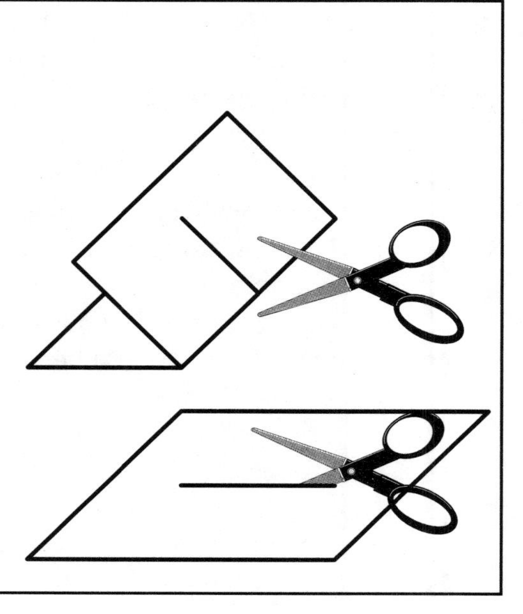

Many of the cut lines extend to the edge of the wheel to making cutting easier for children. When the lines do not extend to the edge, the best way to cut is by following these steps:

1. Loosely curve or bend the paper in half at a right angle to the line to be cut, and then "snip" along the line, just to get the cut started.
2. Re-open the paper to its former flat state, and insert the tip of the scissors into the slit snipped in step 1.
3. Carefully cut along the solid line to the end.

Farm Animals, Zoo Animals, Clothes, Number Facts, and **Snack Surprise** have "flap" windows. Show children how to cut out these windows and fold along the dashed lines to create a flap effect.

Be sure to demonstrate how to use the wheels once they are constructed. Show your students how to turn the wheels so the images on the bottom wheel appear in the windows. Some of the wheels include match-up lines or numbers to make this easier. The wheels work best if the bottom wheel is turned while the top wheel is held in place. All story wheels are designed to be turned clockwise so the story sequence is correct.

Ideas for Using the Wheels

Children will love cutting out, coloring, and using their own wheels. But you may also want to make sturdy versions of the wheels for learning centers. To do this, copy and cut out the wheels you want to make. Then glue them onto tag board or recycled manila folders. Use an Exacto knife to cut through the tag board. You can then color the wheels, laminate them, and insert the paper fastener.

You may also want to include wheels as part of a take-home "thematic backpack." The backpack can also contain books and a class journal for each child to contribute to when they take the backpack home.

Your students can use the blank wheels in many different ways. The one on pages 63-64 works well for reinforcing vocabulary. Children can write (or dictate to you) words to put in the small window. Then they can either draw or cut pictures from magazines that illustrate the word in the larger window. Invite them to use the blank story wheel (page 61-62) to retell stories you've read to them. Or they can use them to create original stories.

Day and Night

Top

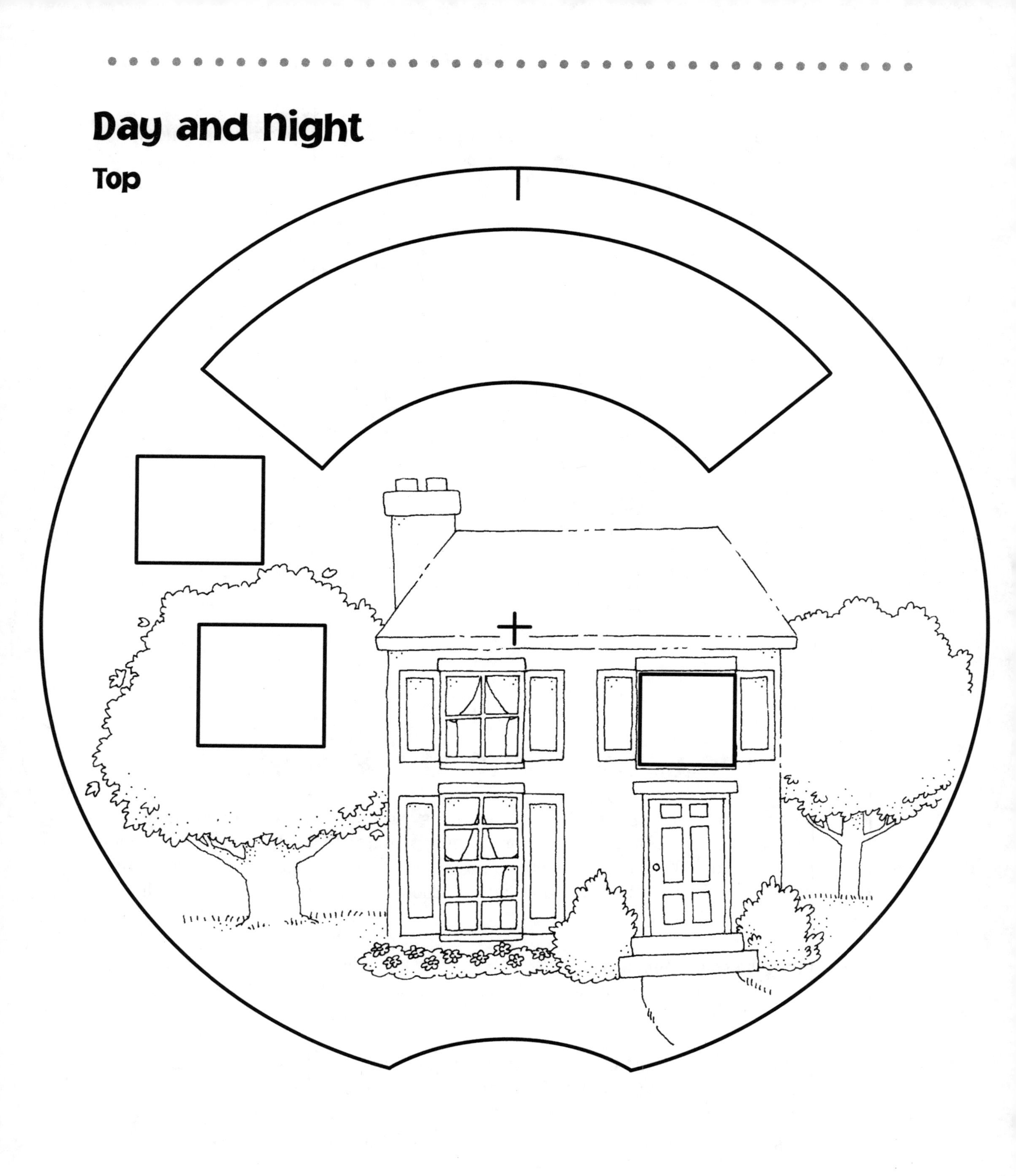

Day and Night

Bottom

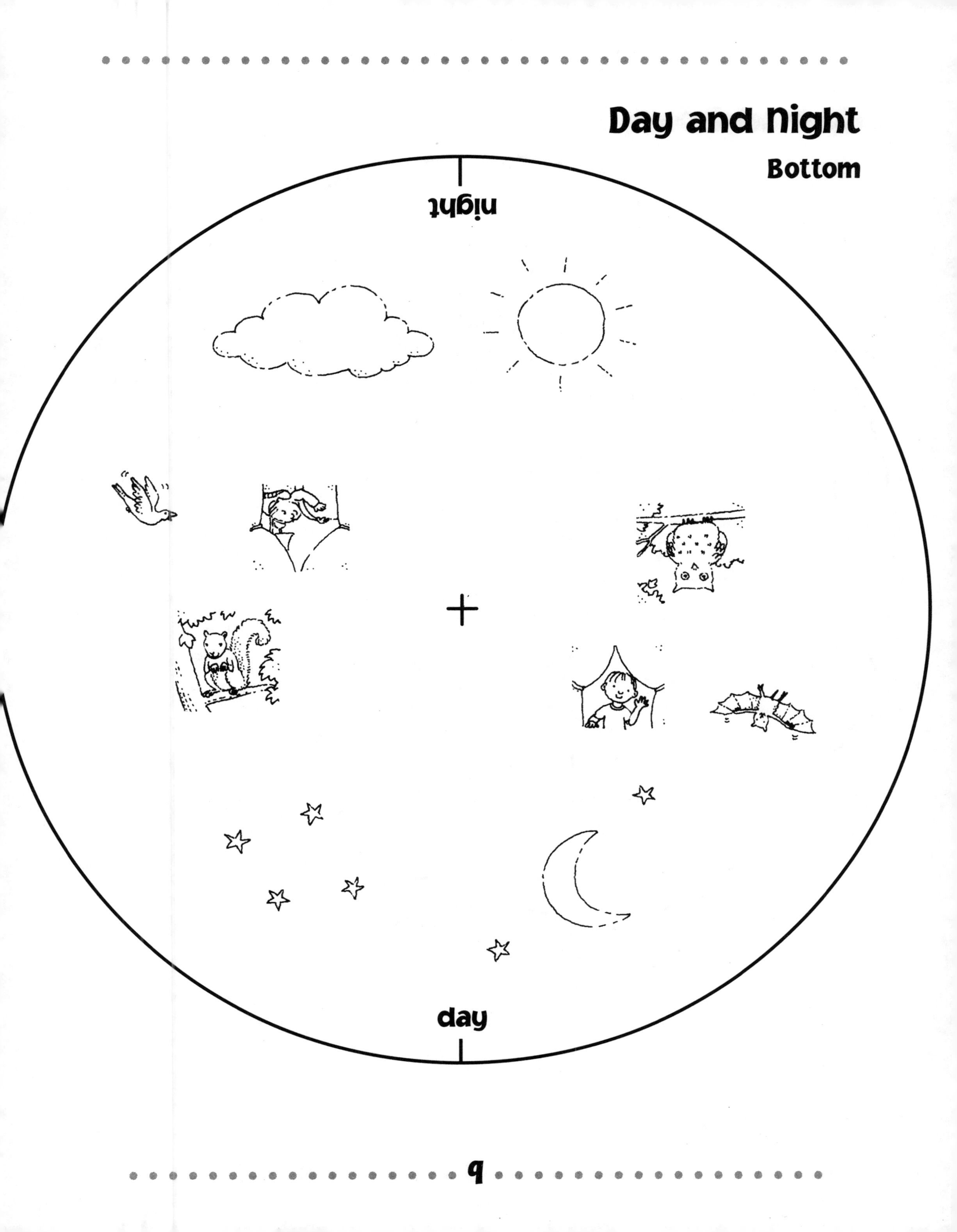

Up and Down

Top

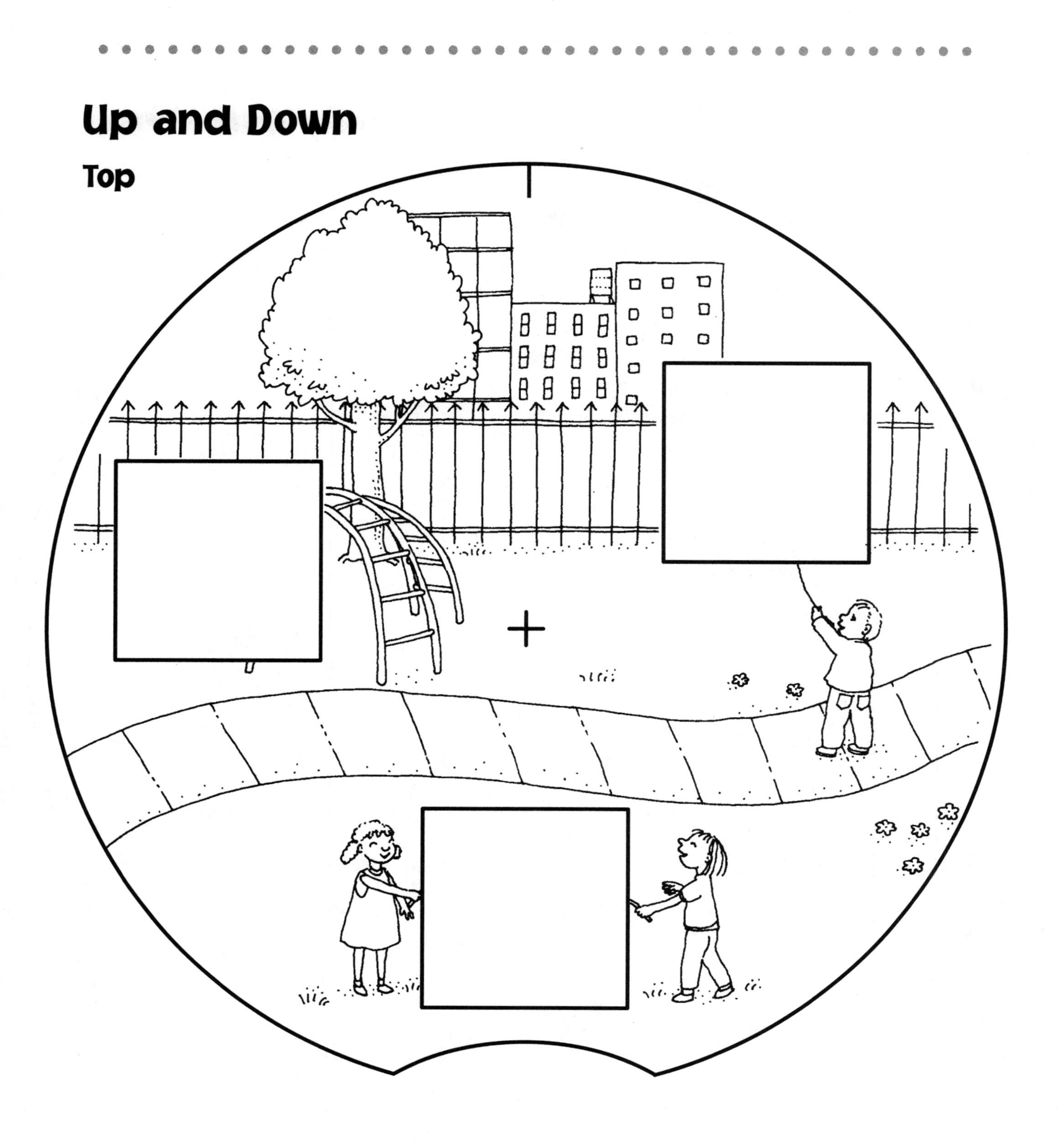

Up and Down

Bottom

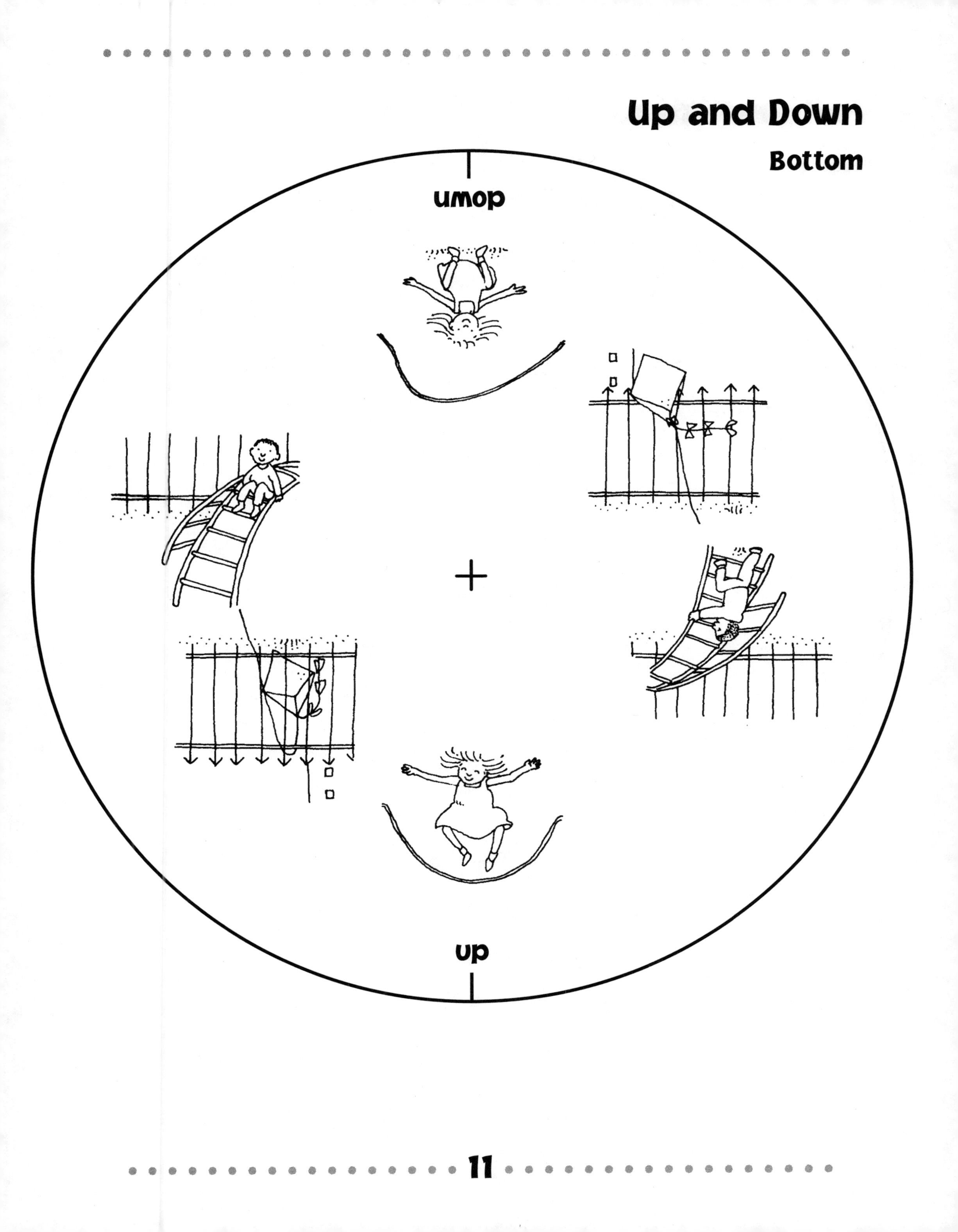

Full and Empty

Top

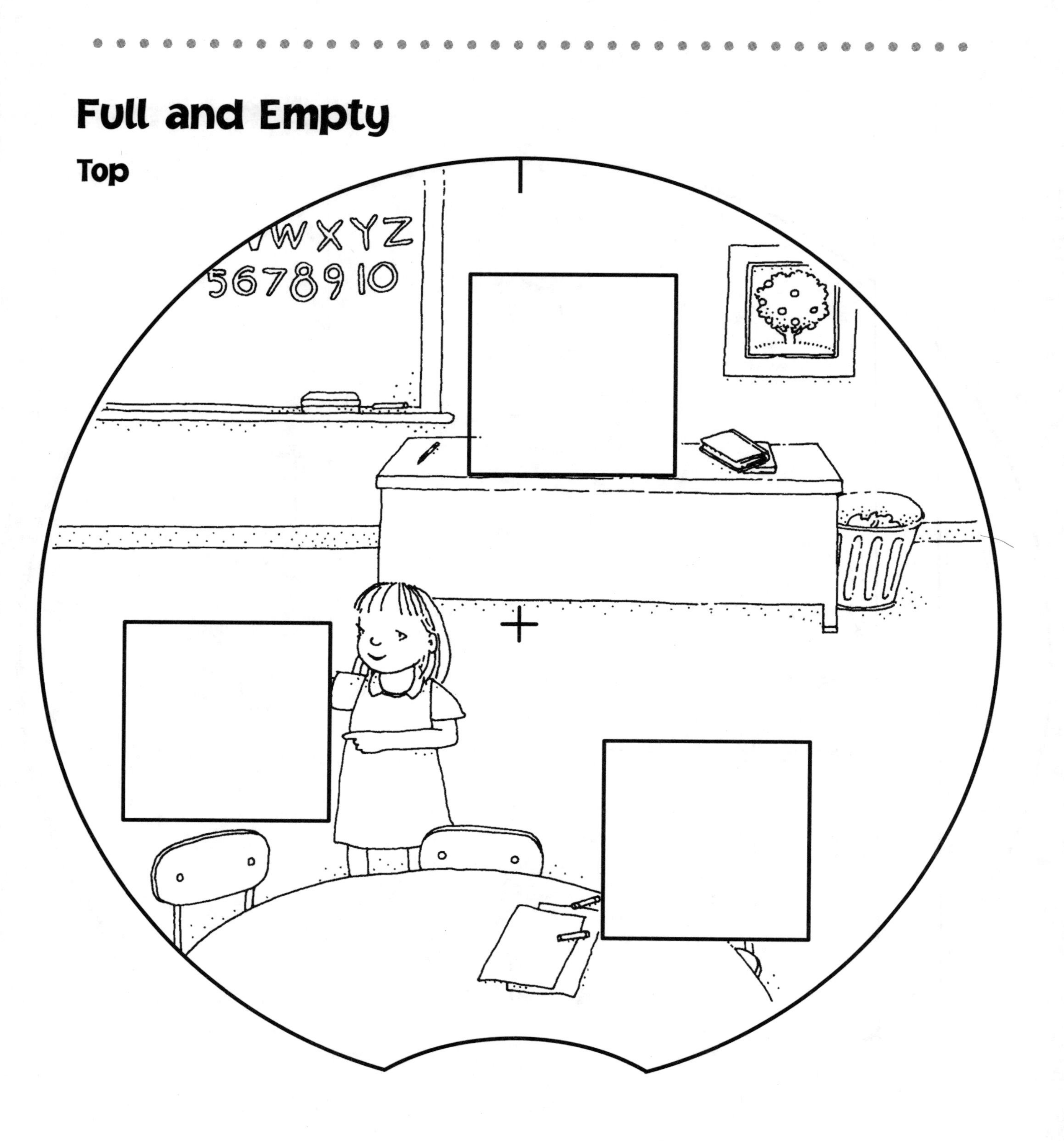

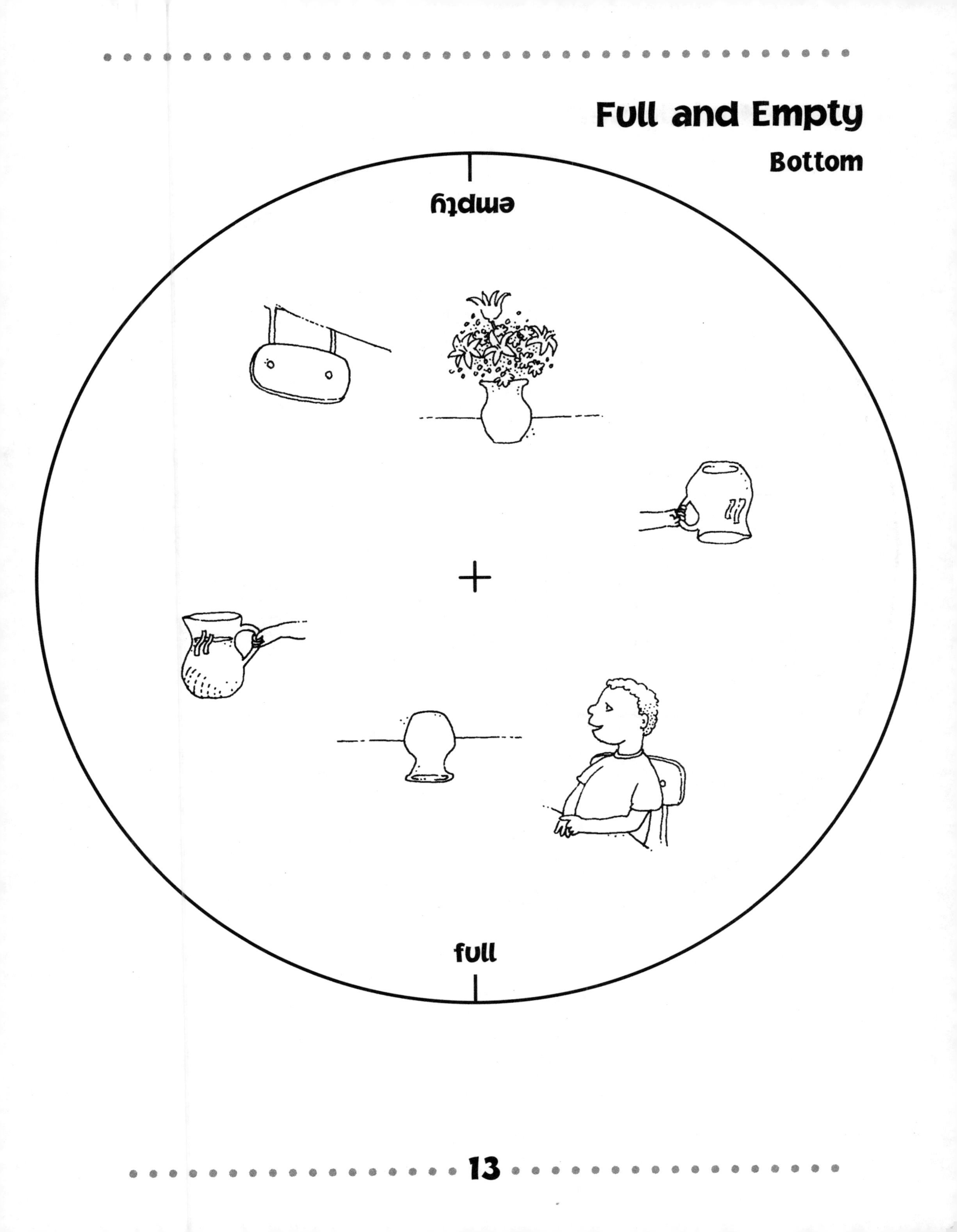
Full and Empty
Bottom
empty
full
13

Open and Closed

Top

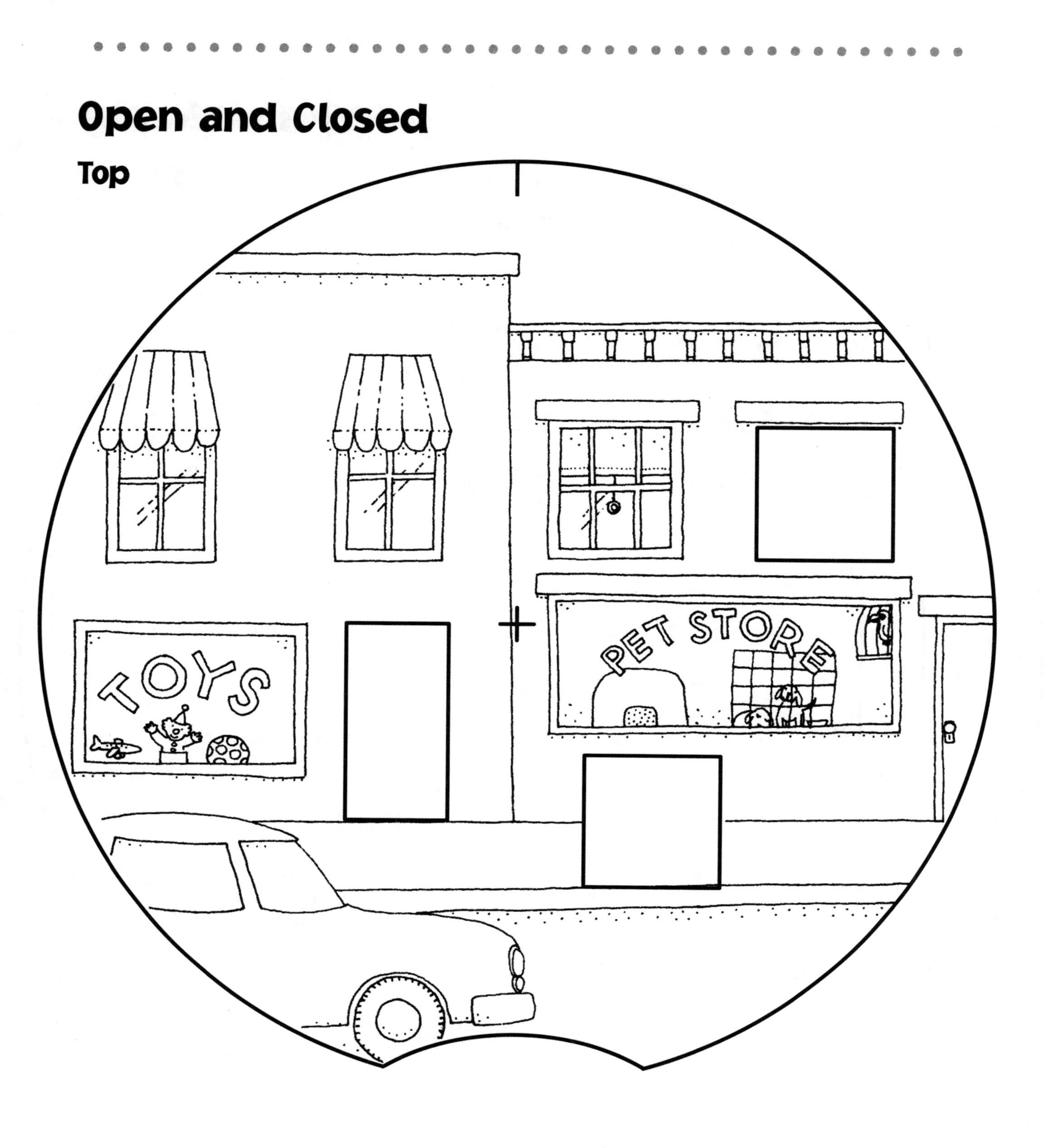

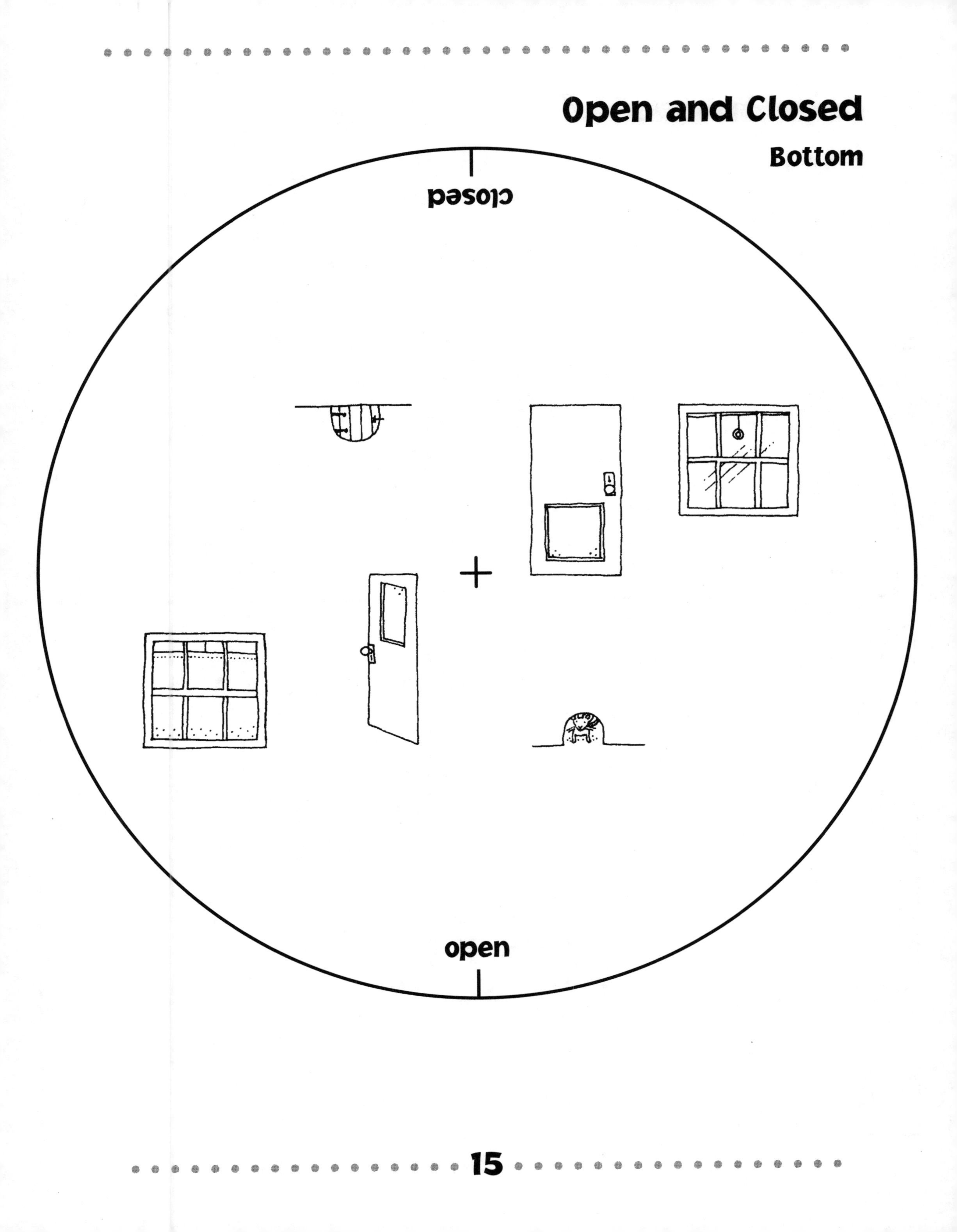
Open and Closed
Bottom
closed
open

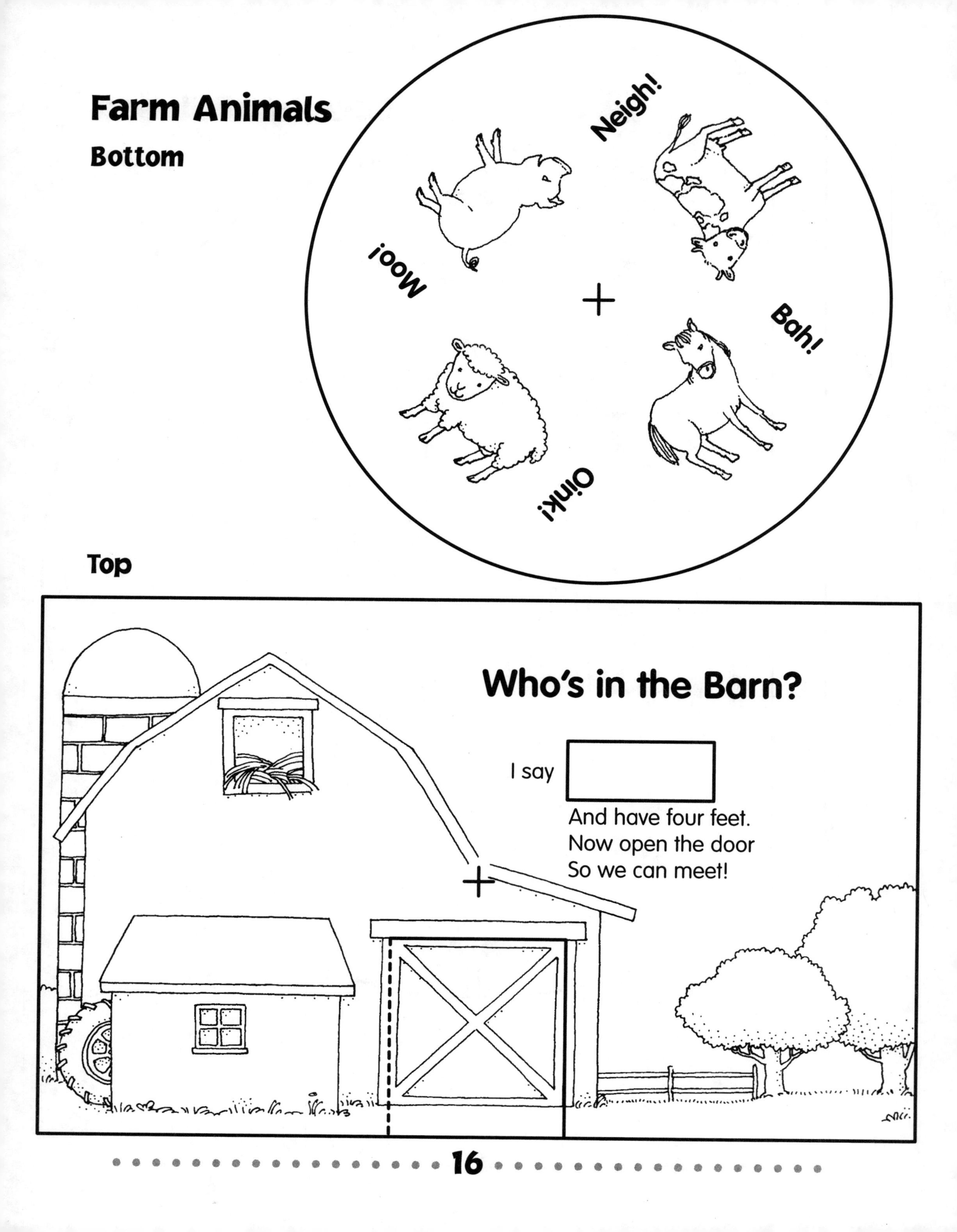
Farm Animals
Bottom
Neigh!
Bah!
Oink!
Moo!
Top
Who's in the Barn?
I say
And have four feet.
Now open the door
So we can meet!
16

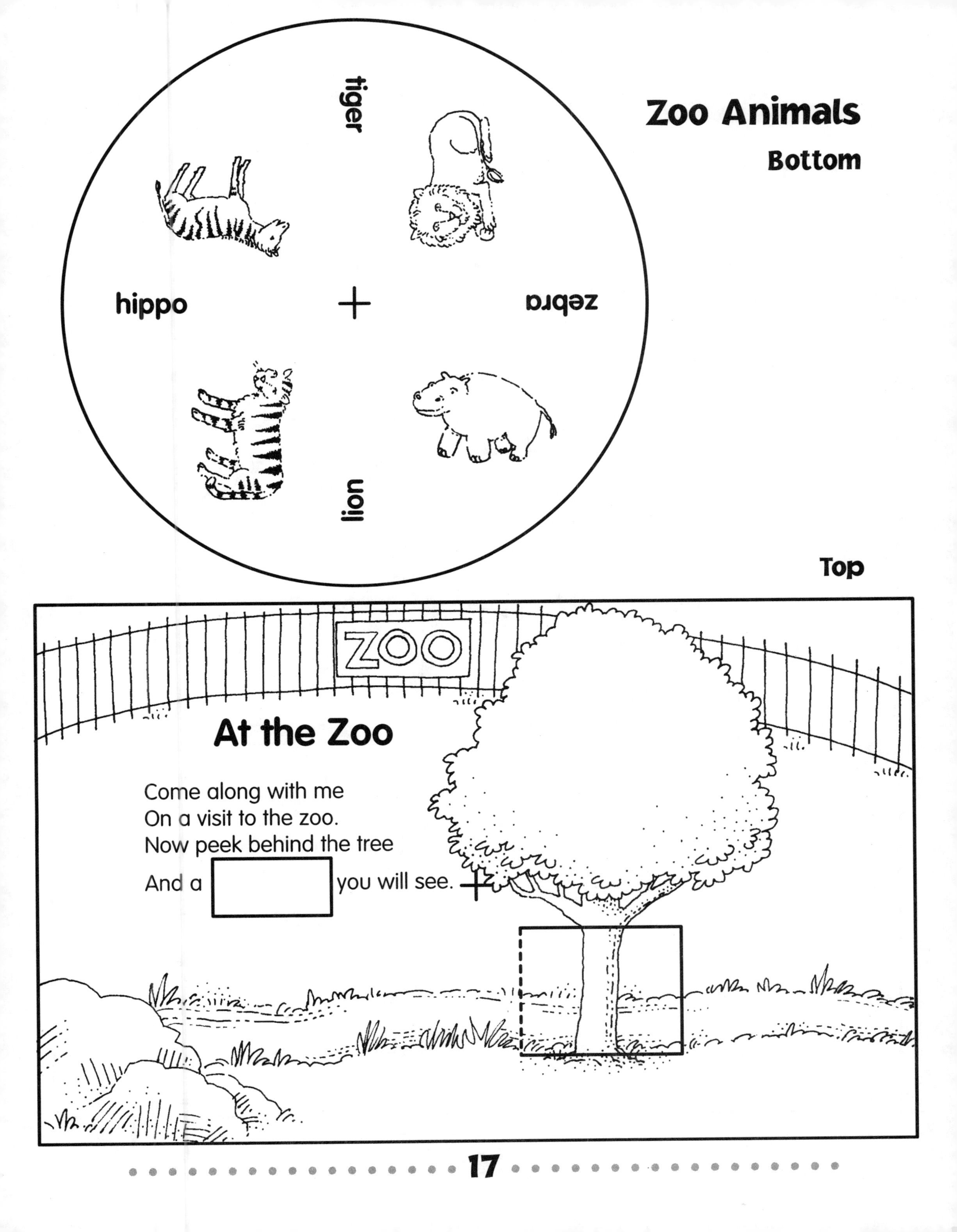
tiger
hippo
zebra
lion
Zoo Animals
Bottom
Top
ZOO
At the Zoo
Come along with me
On a visit to the zoo.
Now peek behind the tree
And a you will see.

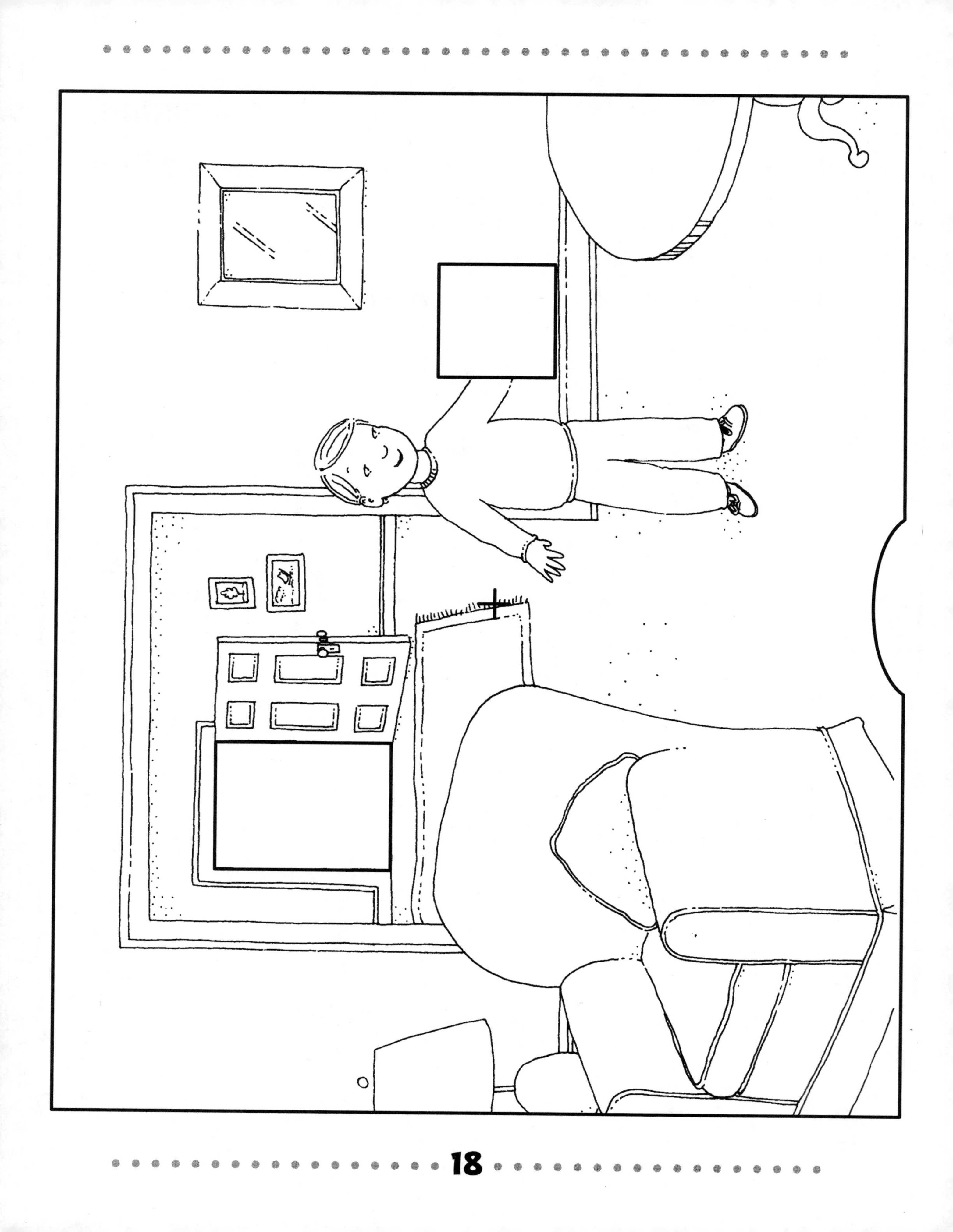

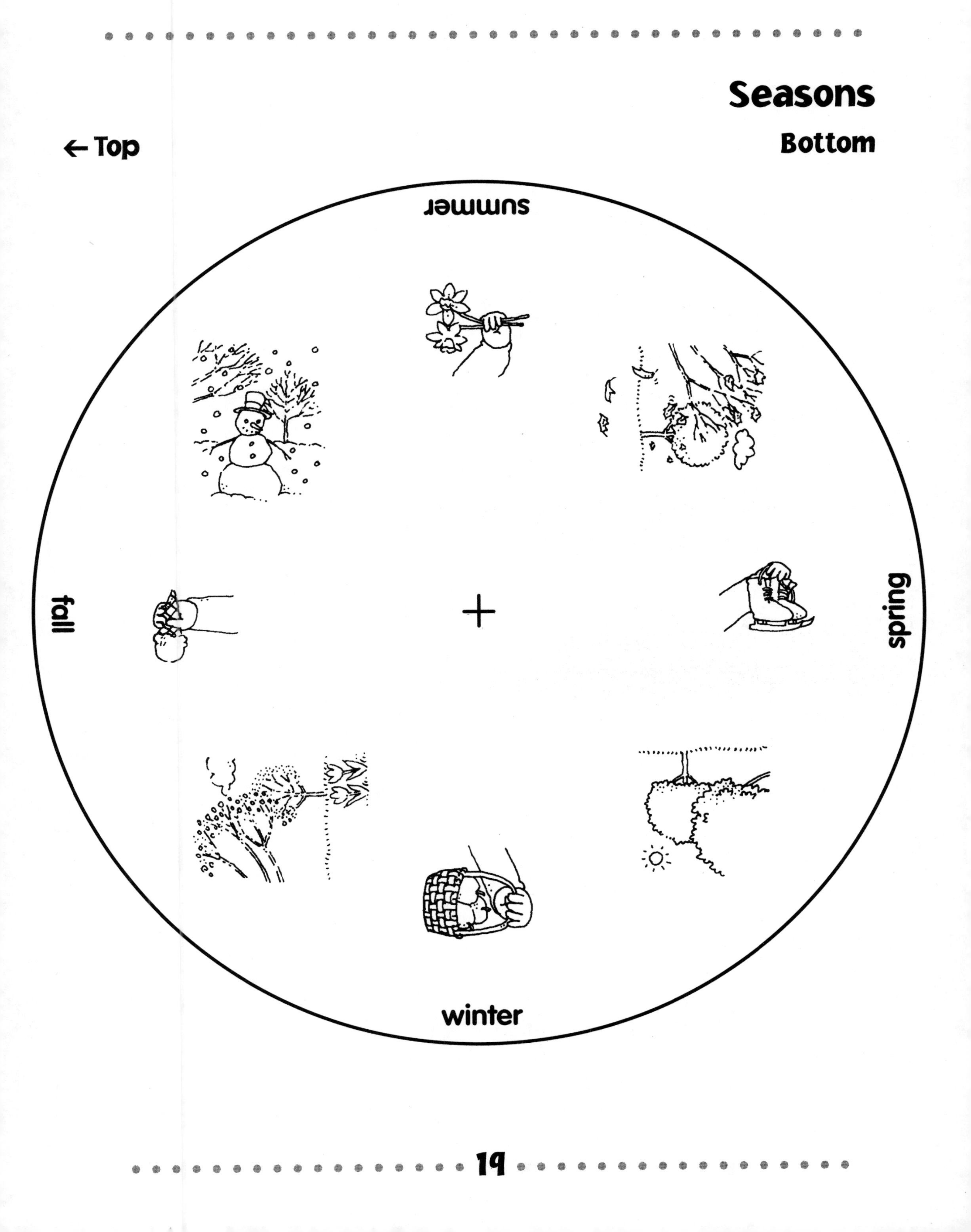
Seasons
← Top
Bottom
summer
fall
spring
winter

Colors

Top

Colors

Bottom

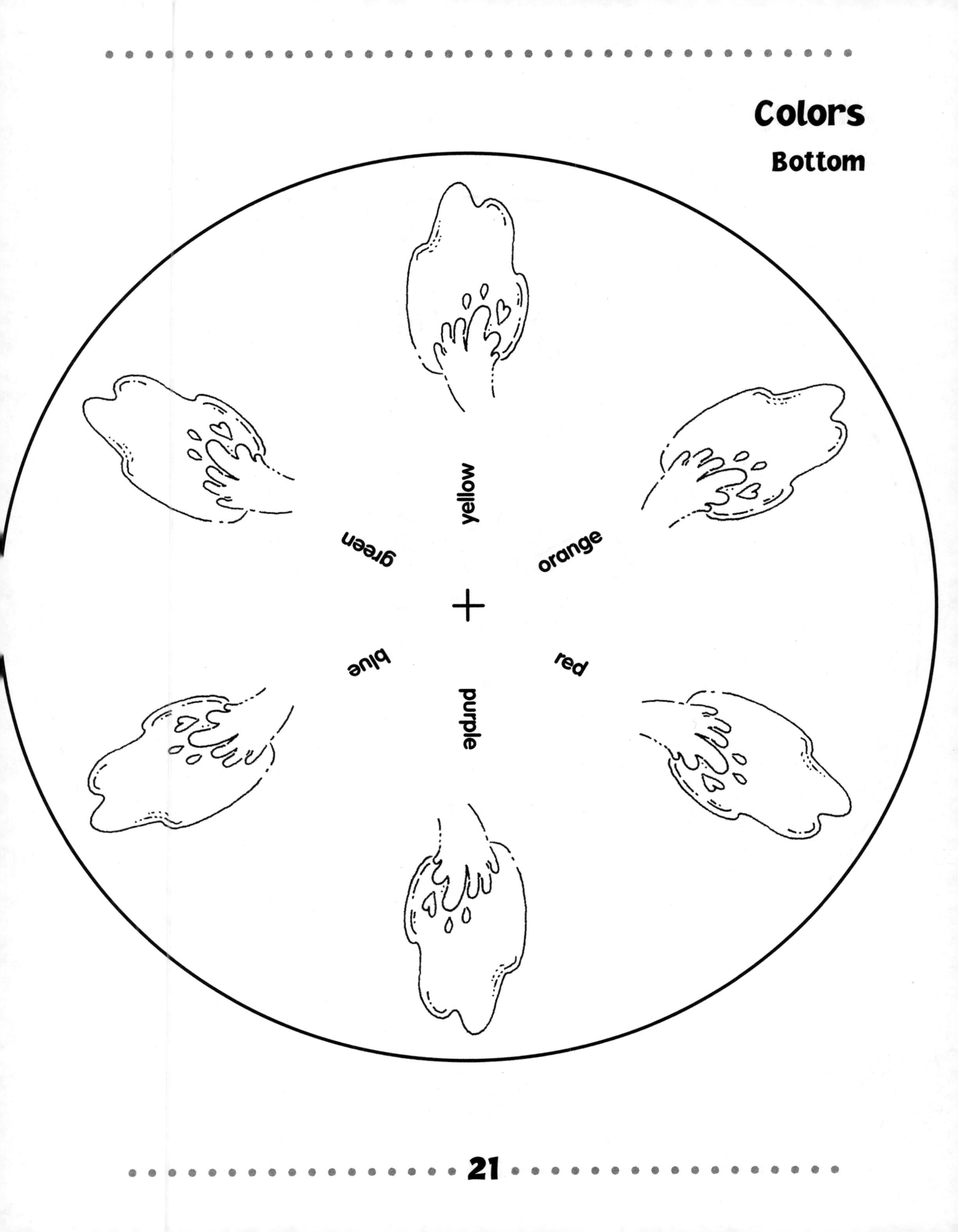

Mixing Colors

Top

Mixing Colors

Bottom

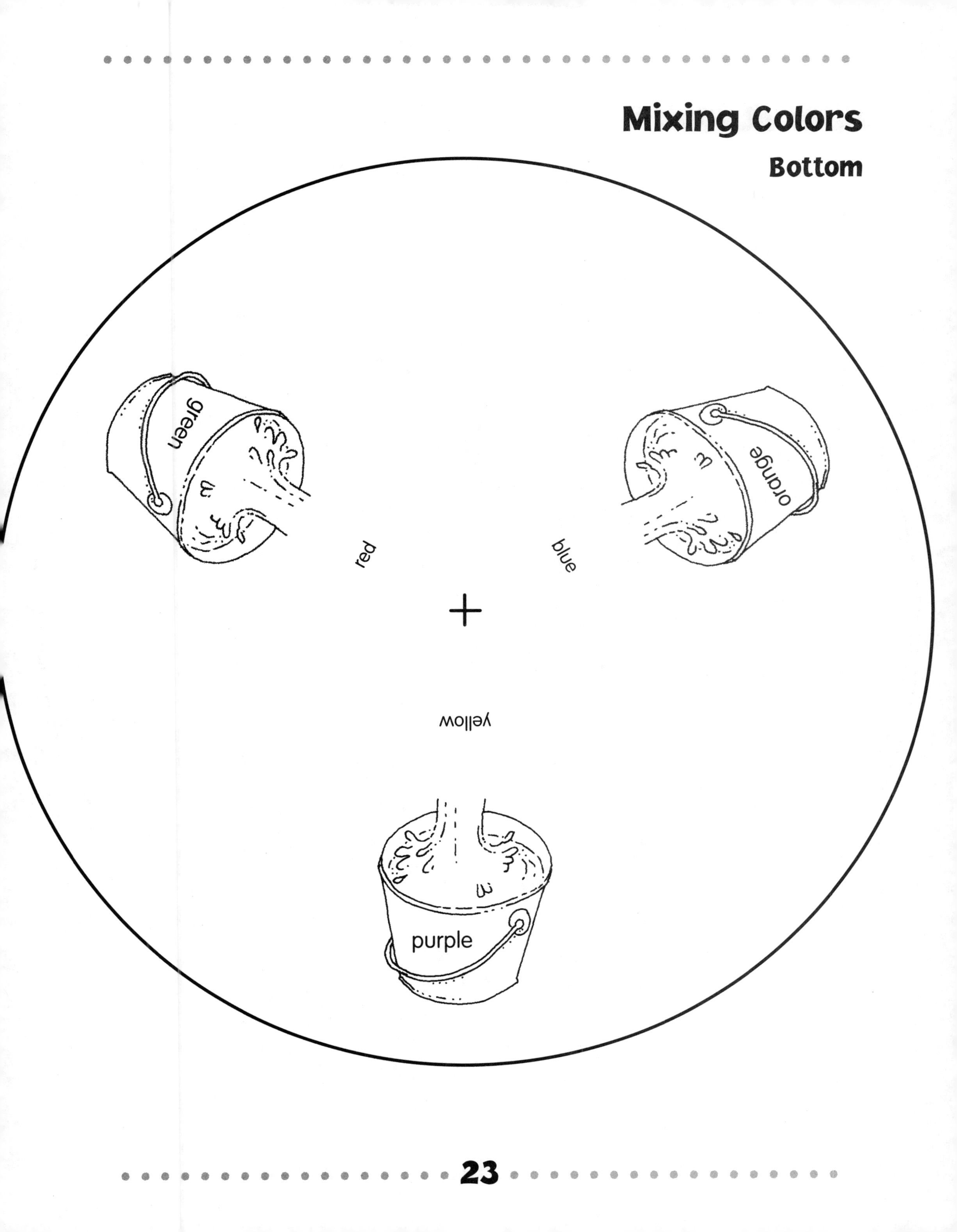

Hats at Work

Top

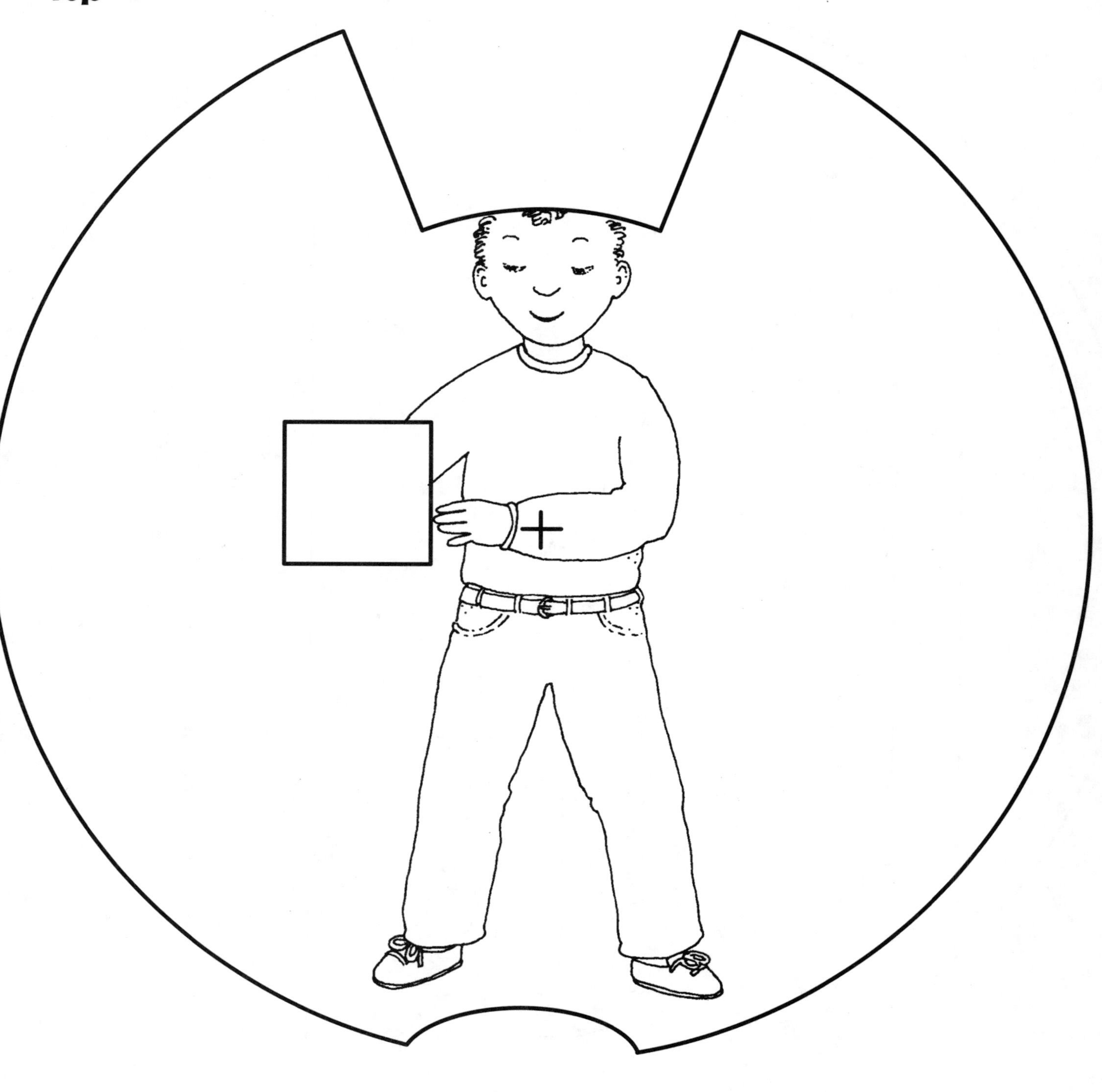

Hats at Work

Bottom

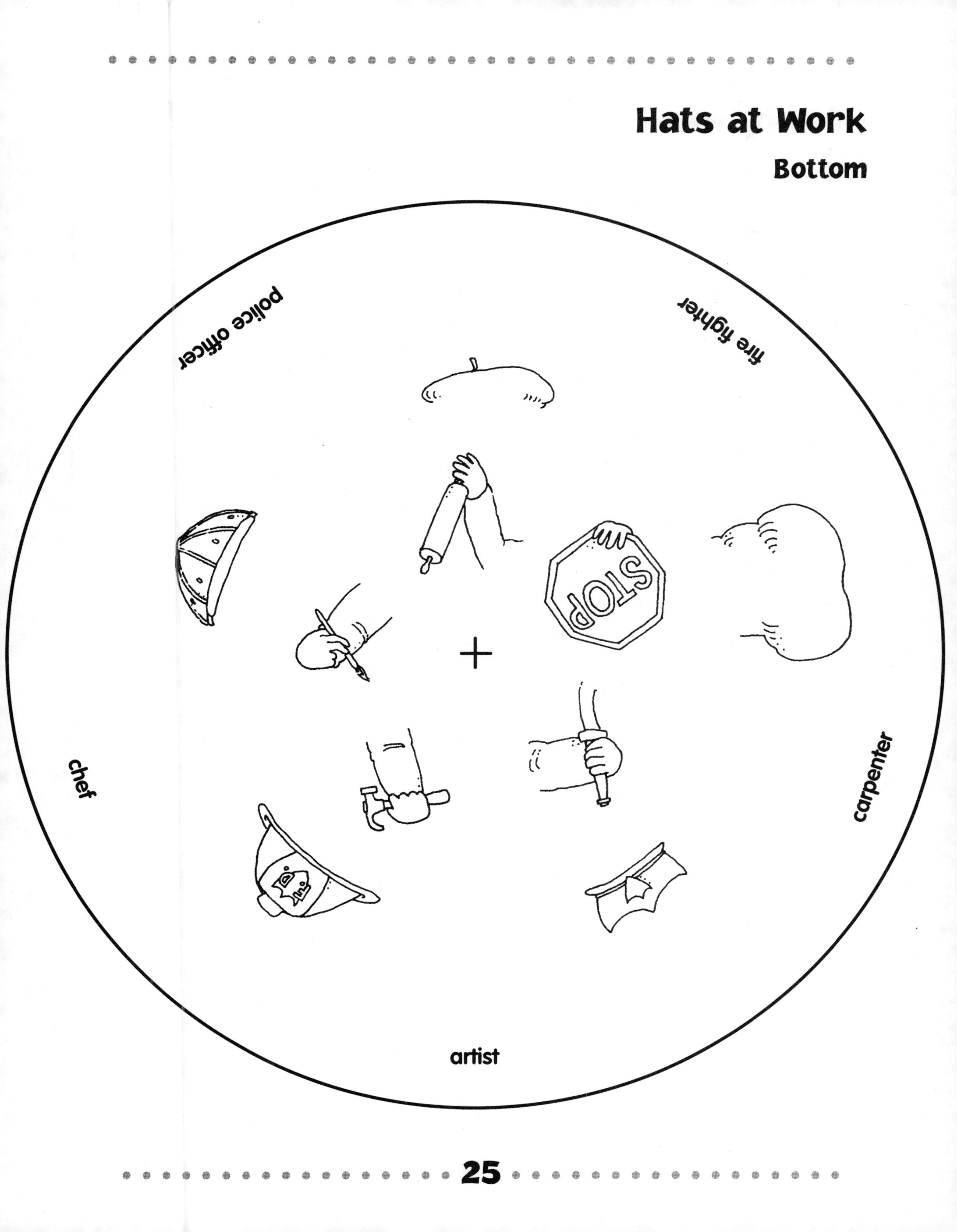

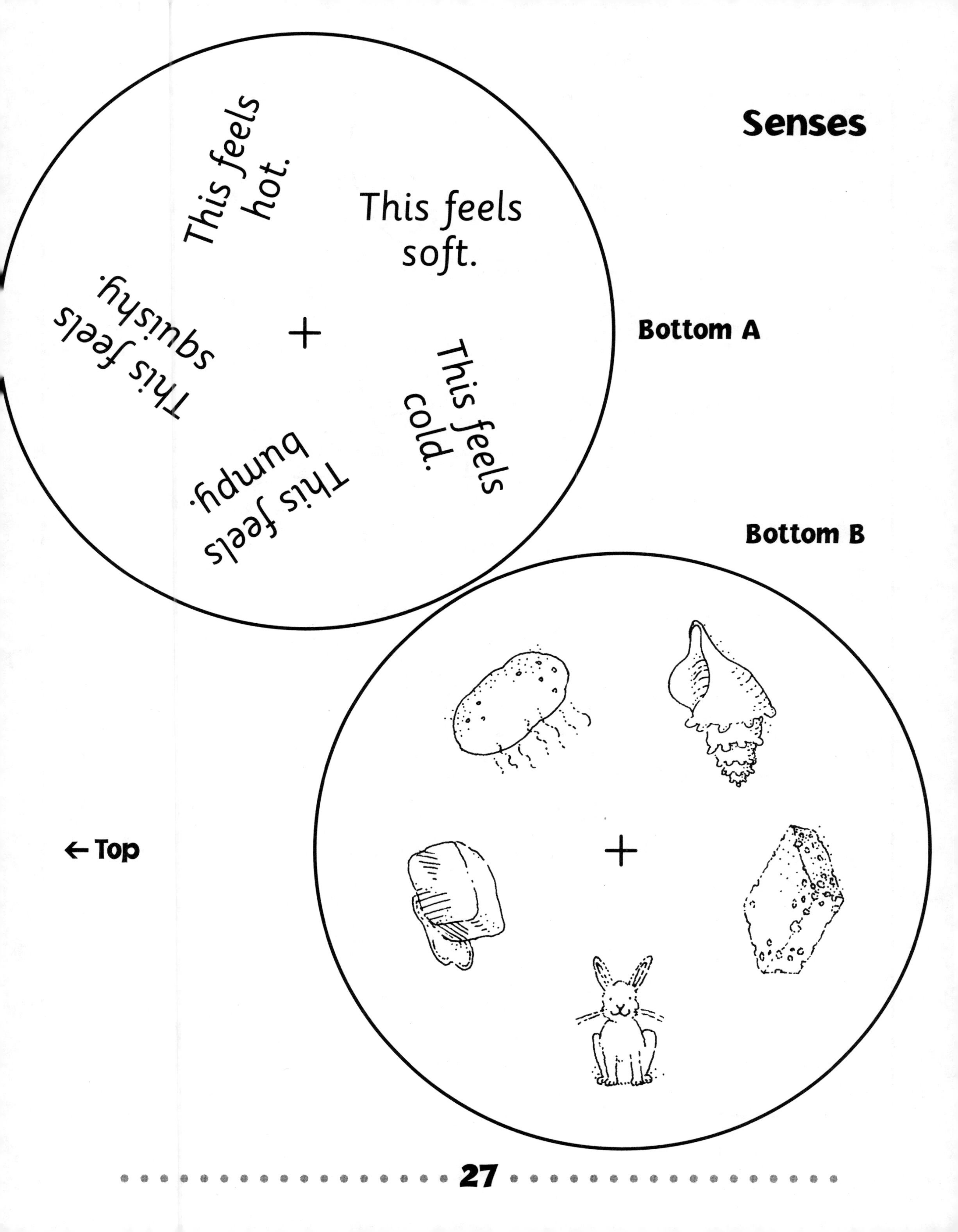
Senses
Bottom A
This feels hot.
This feels soft.
This feels squishy.
This feels cold.
This feels bumpy.
Bottom B
← Top

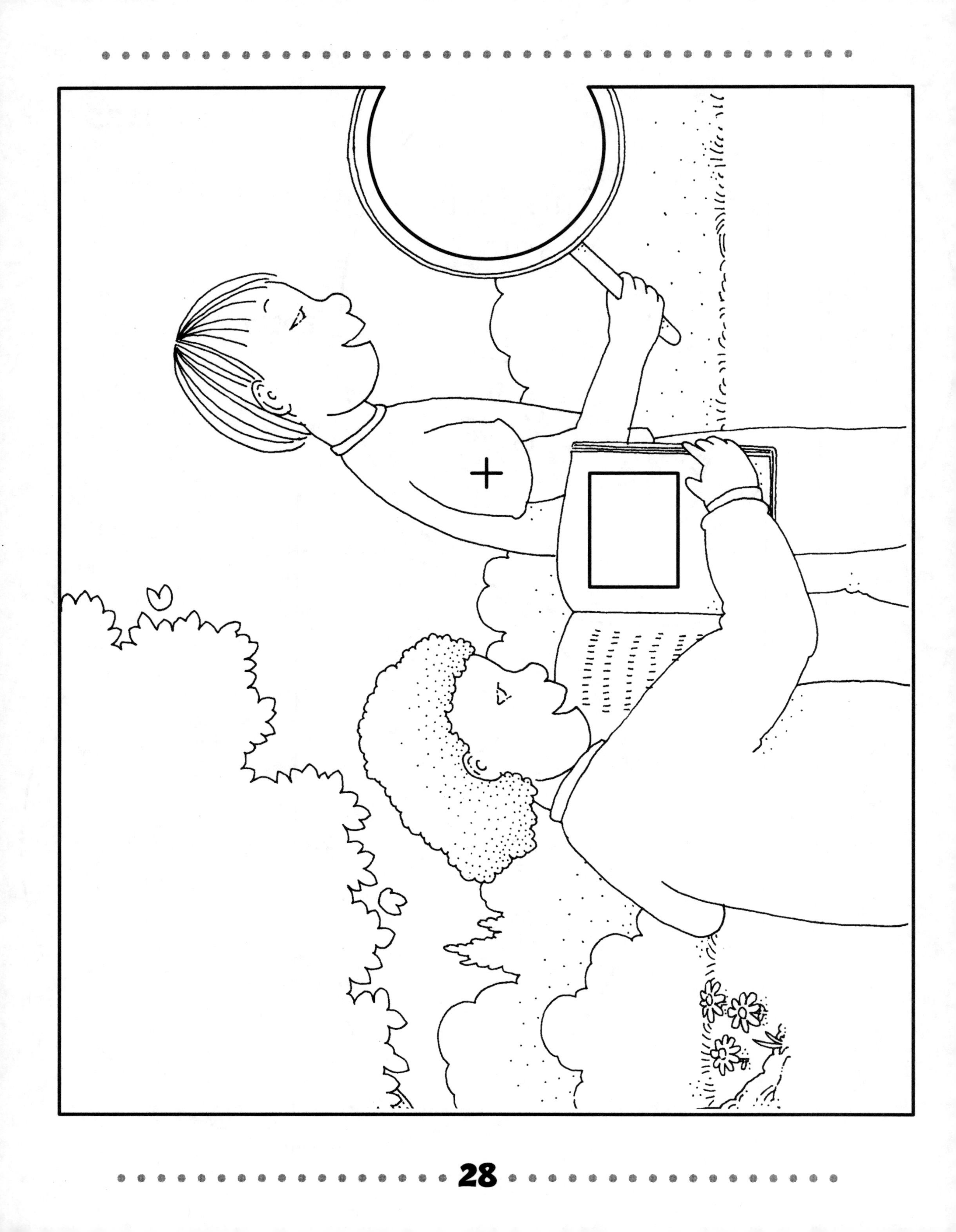

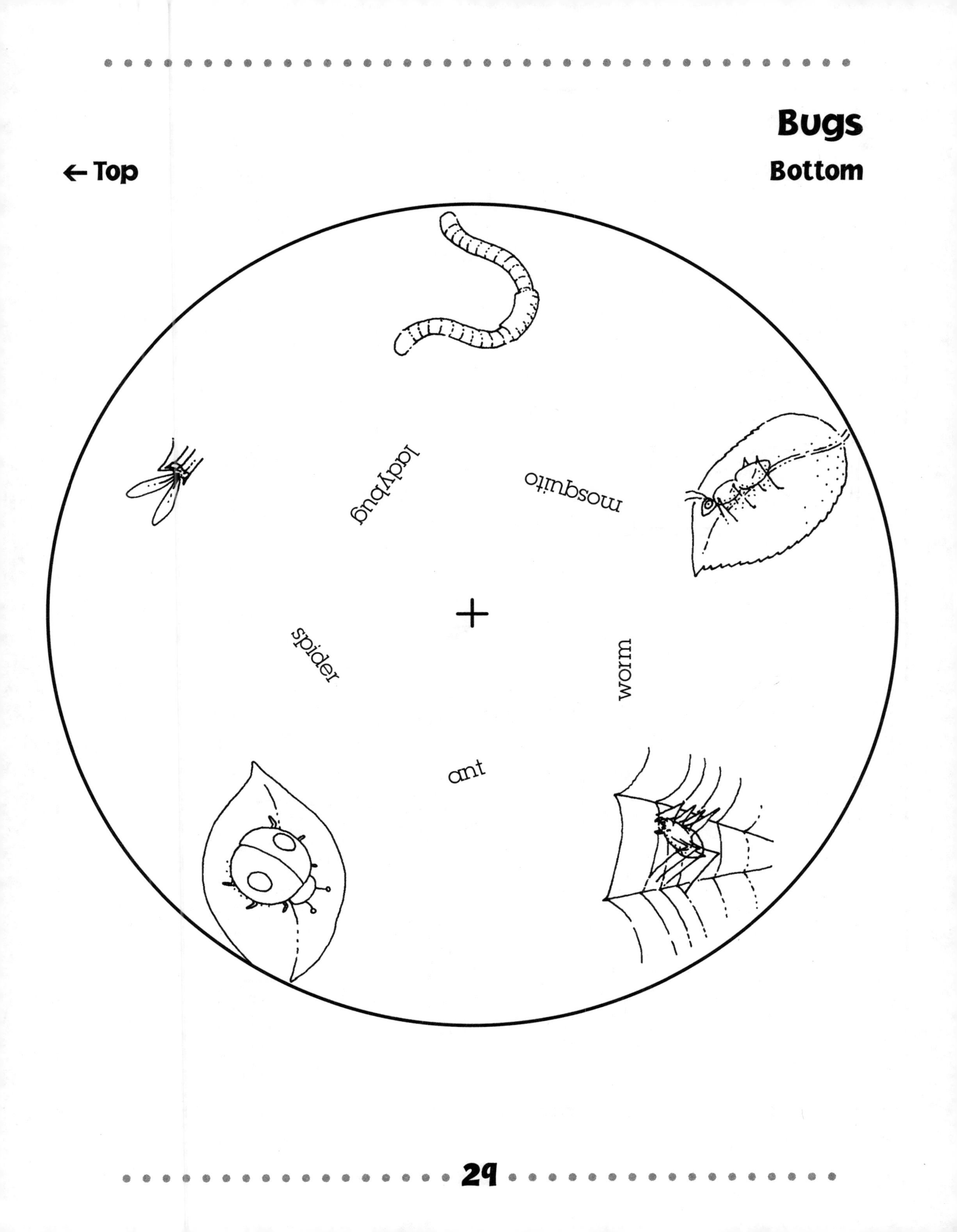
Bugs
← Top
Bottom
ladybug
mosquito
spider
worm
ant

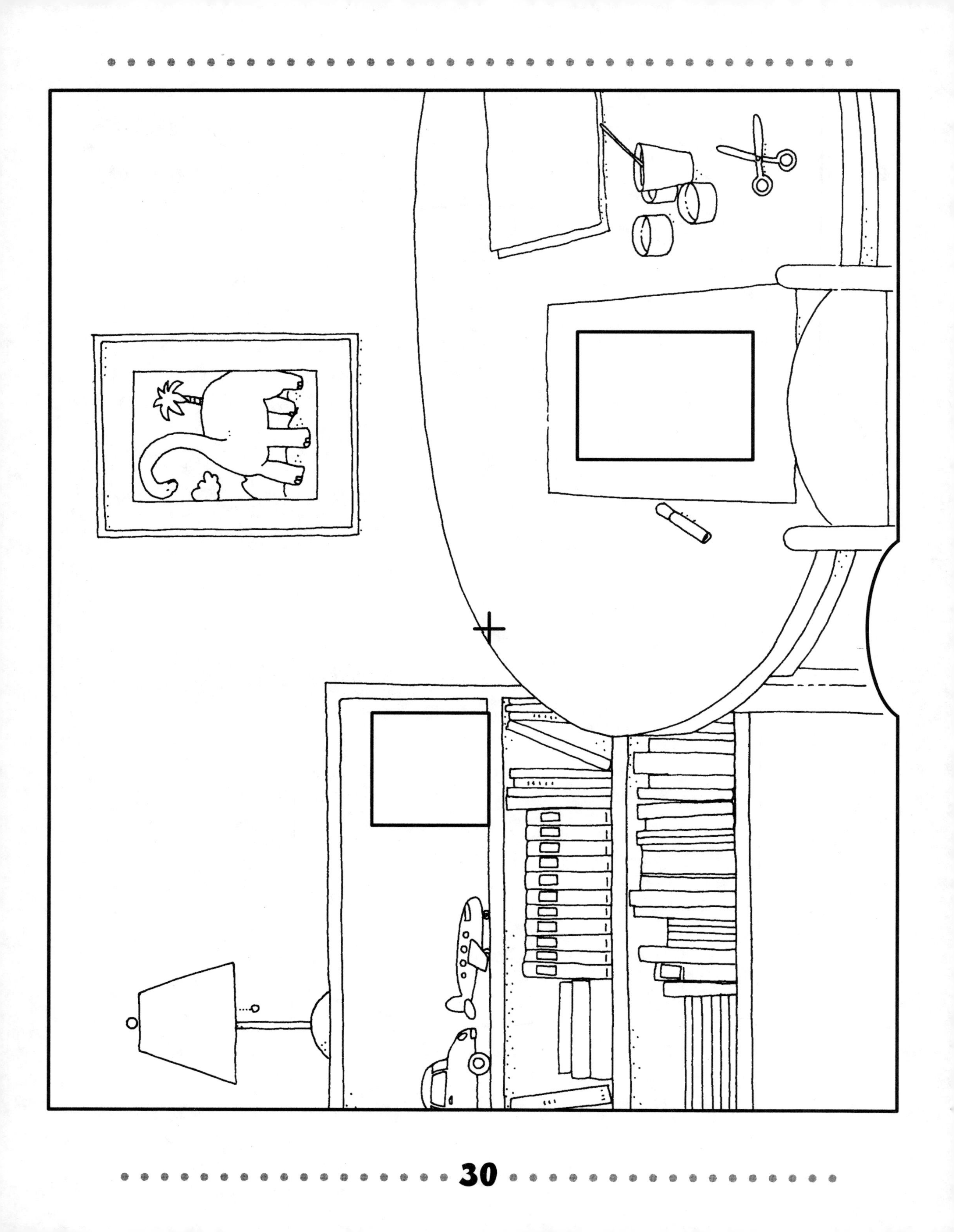

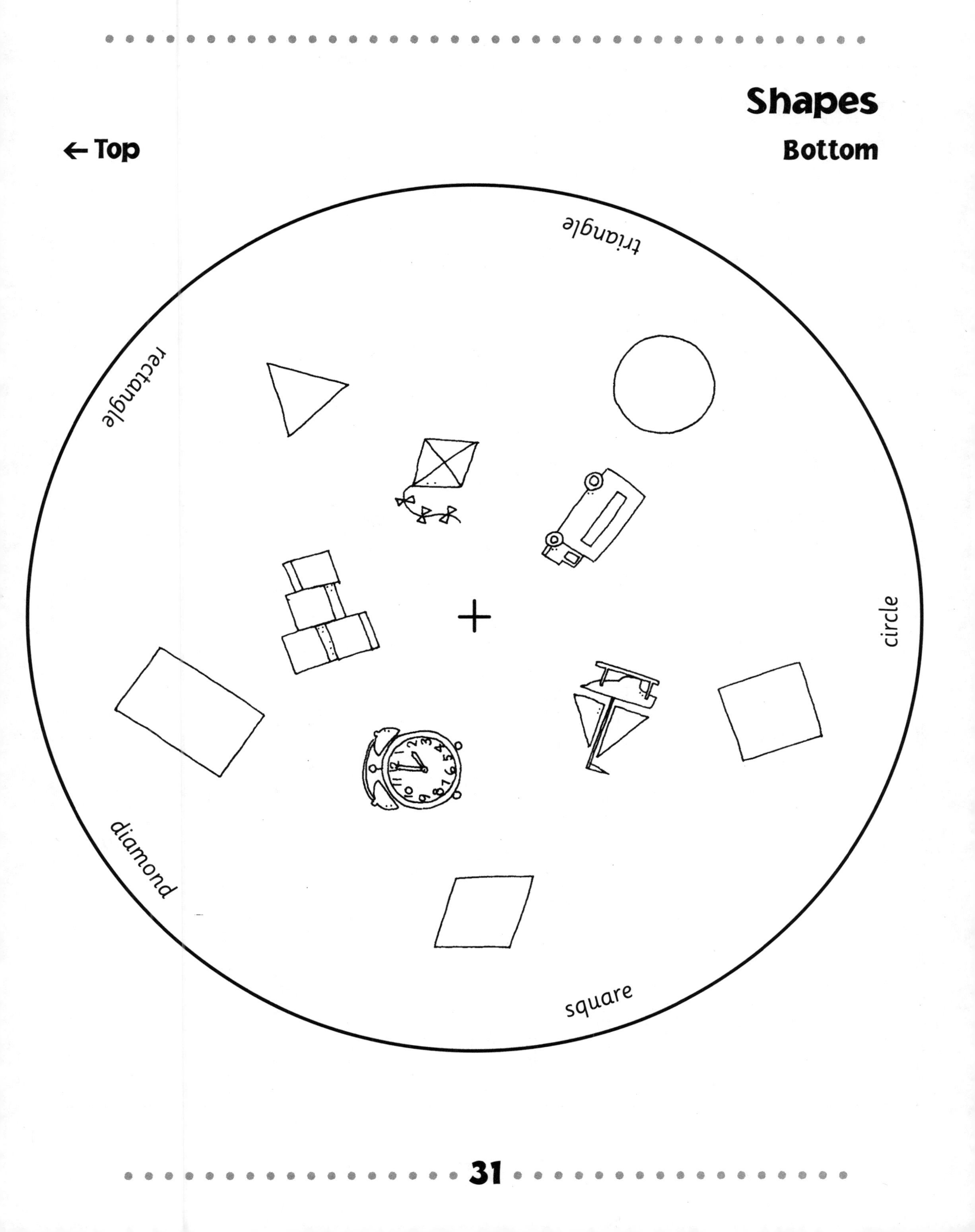
Shapes
← Top
Bottom
triangle
rectangle
circle
diamond
square

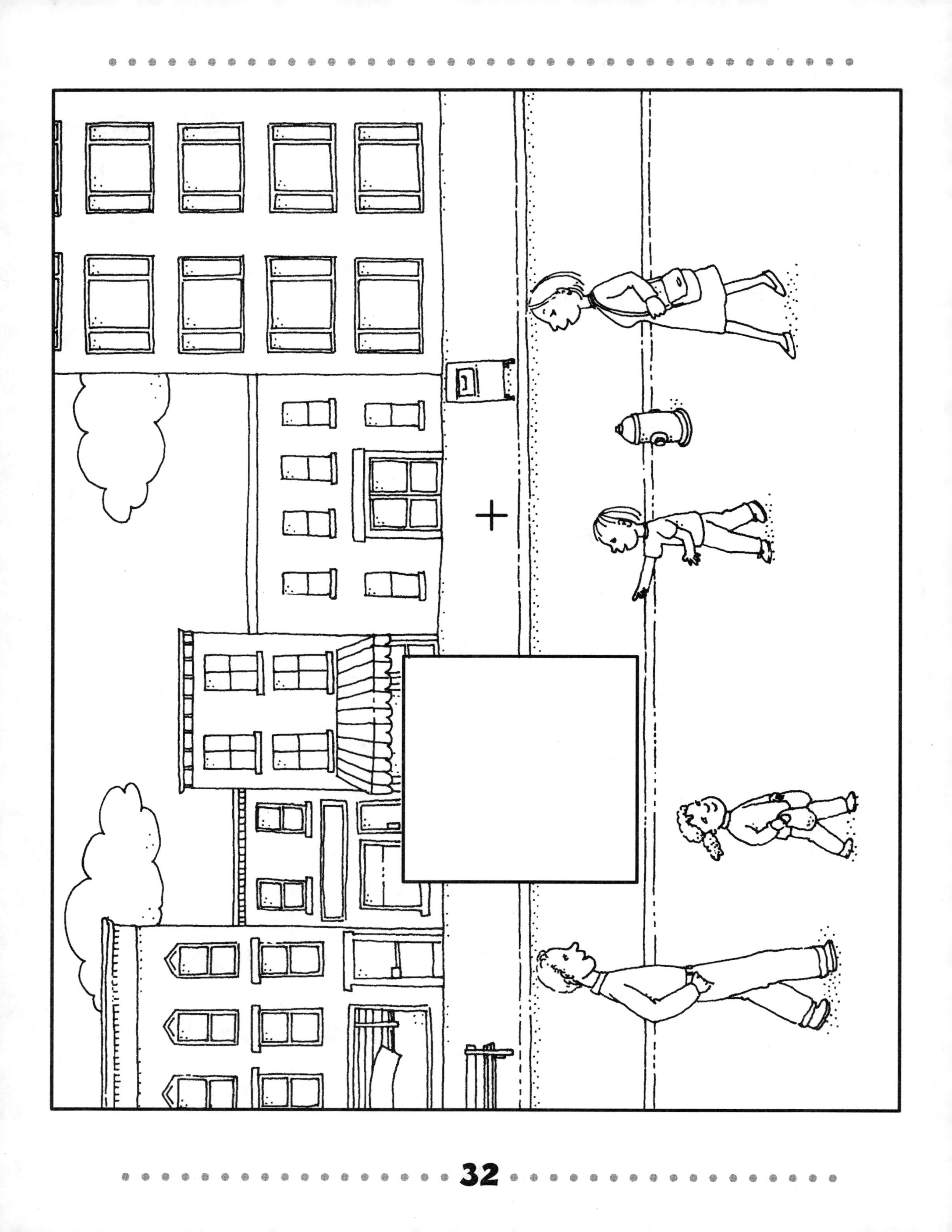

← Top

Bottom

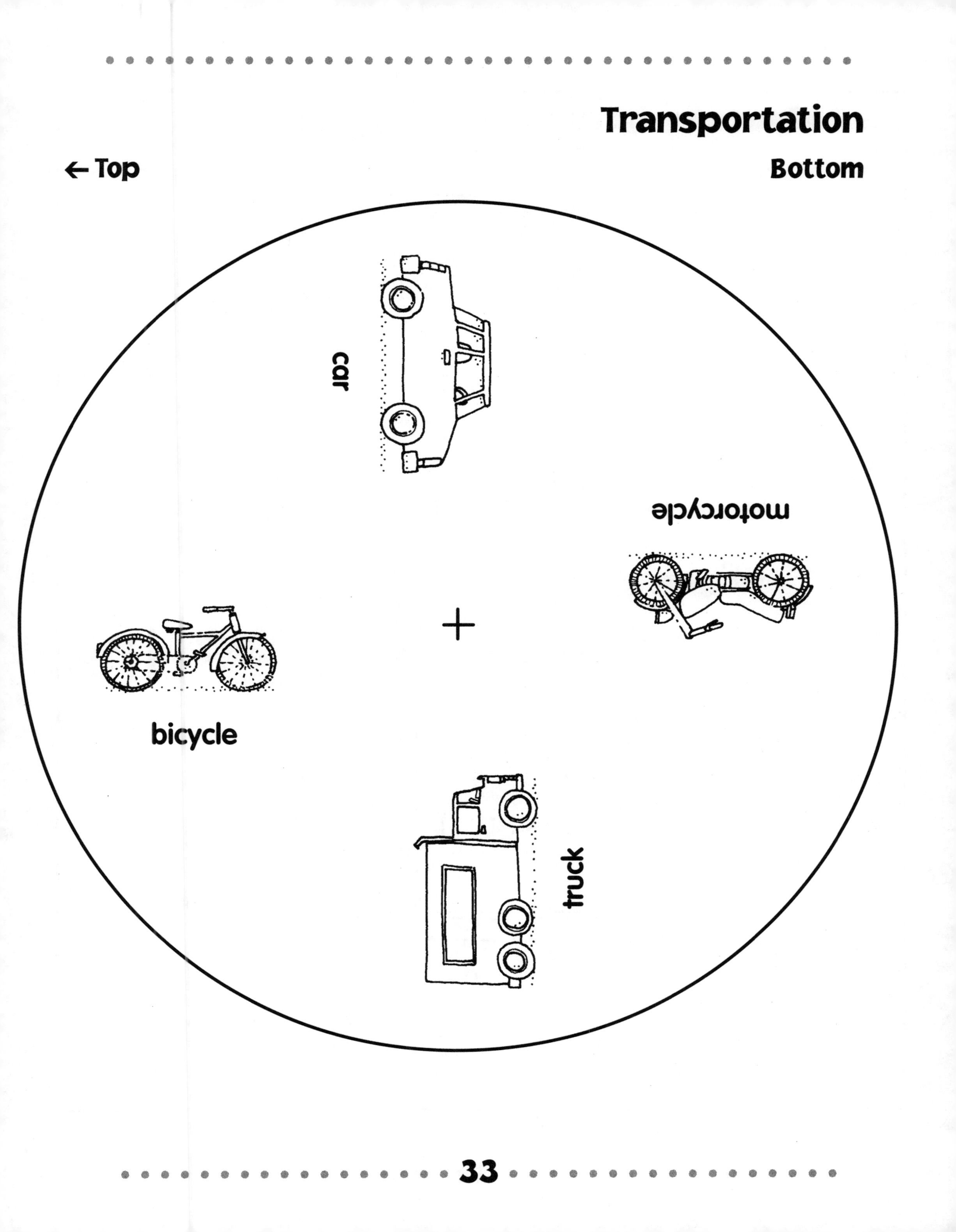

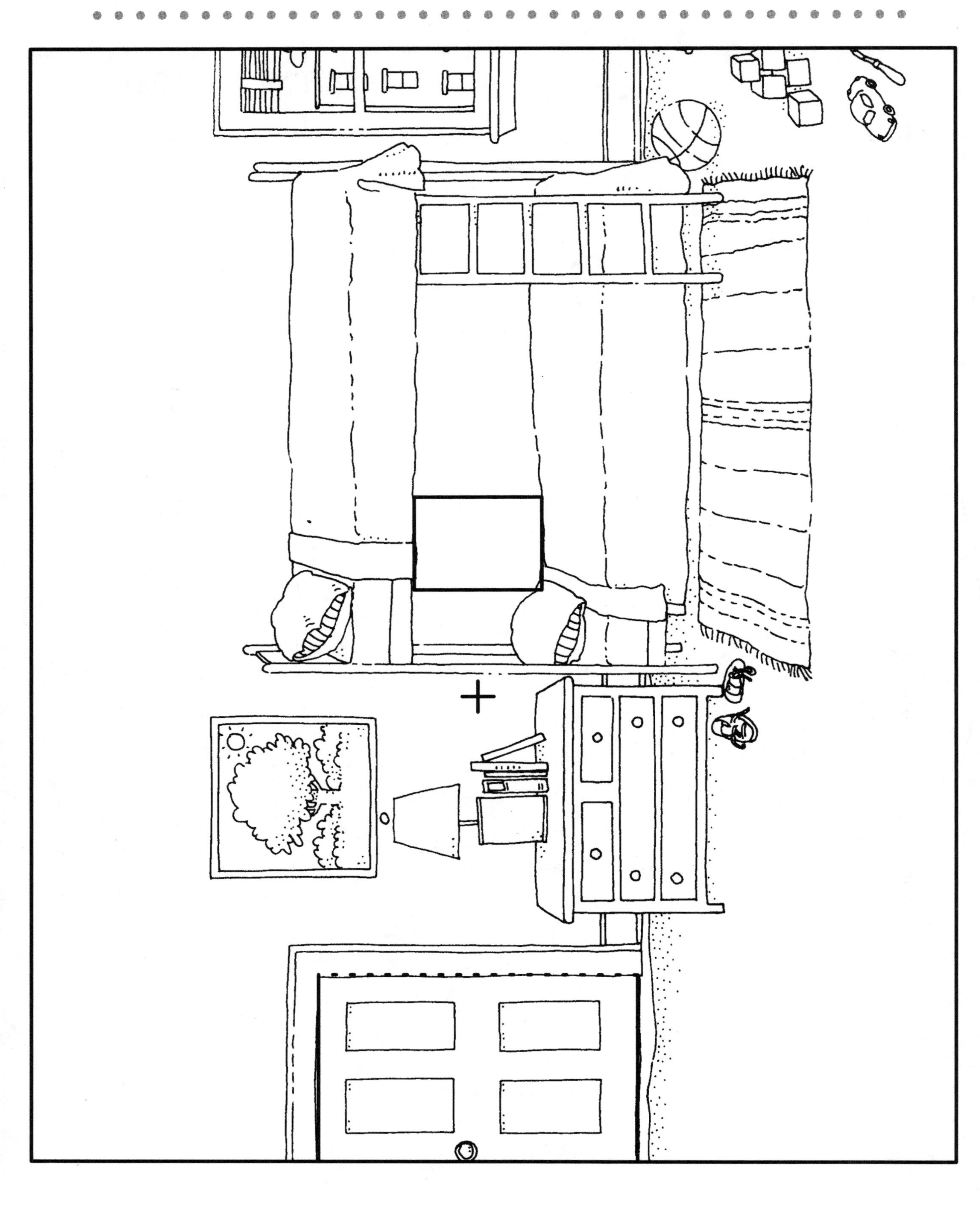

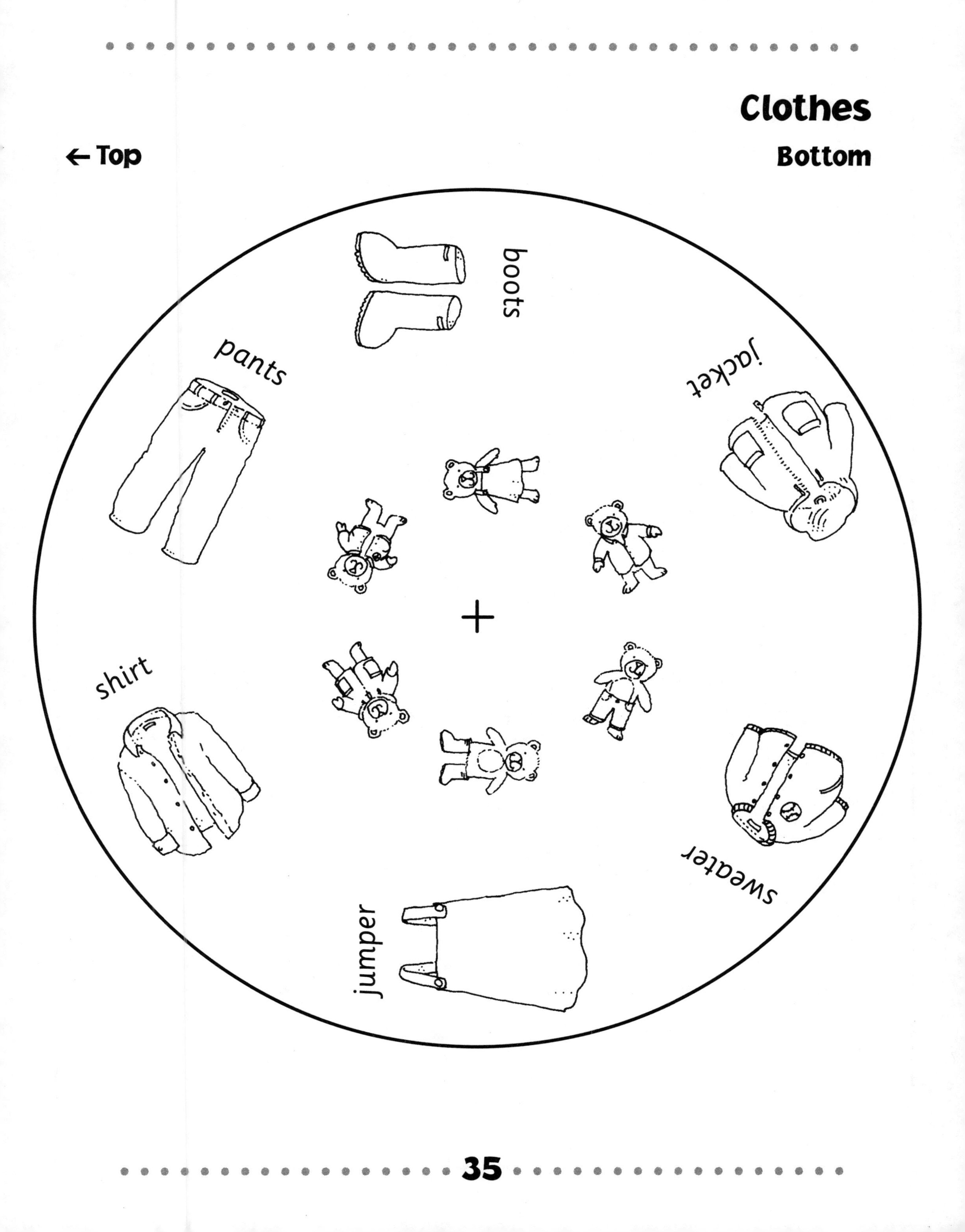
Clothes
← Top
Bottom
boots
pants
jacket
shirt
sweater
jumper

I wonder what I have for snack today?

Snack Surprise

← Top

Bottom

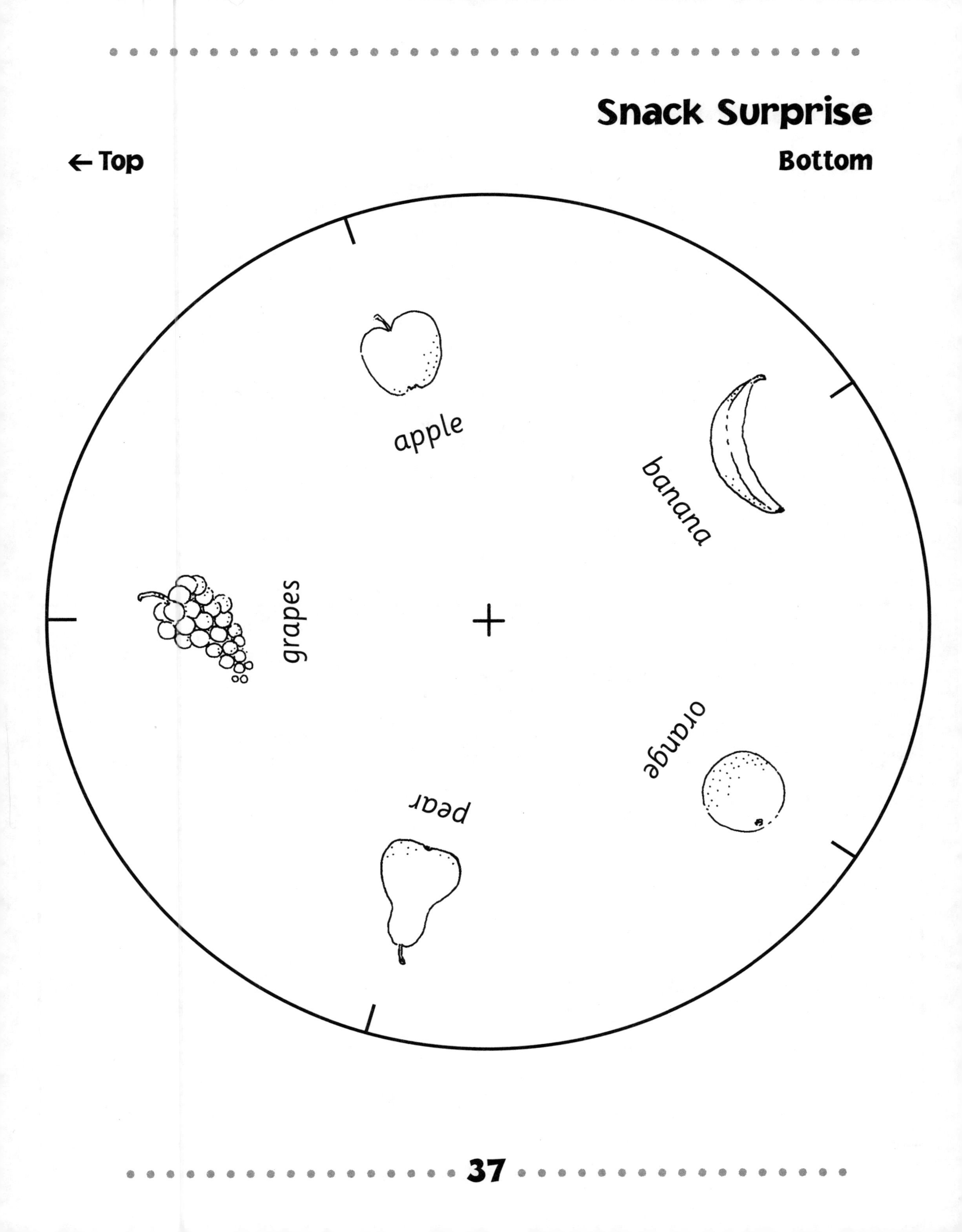

Story Wheel:
Little
Miss Muffet

Story Wheel:
Jack and Jill

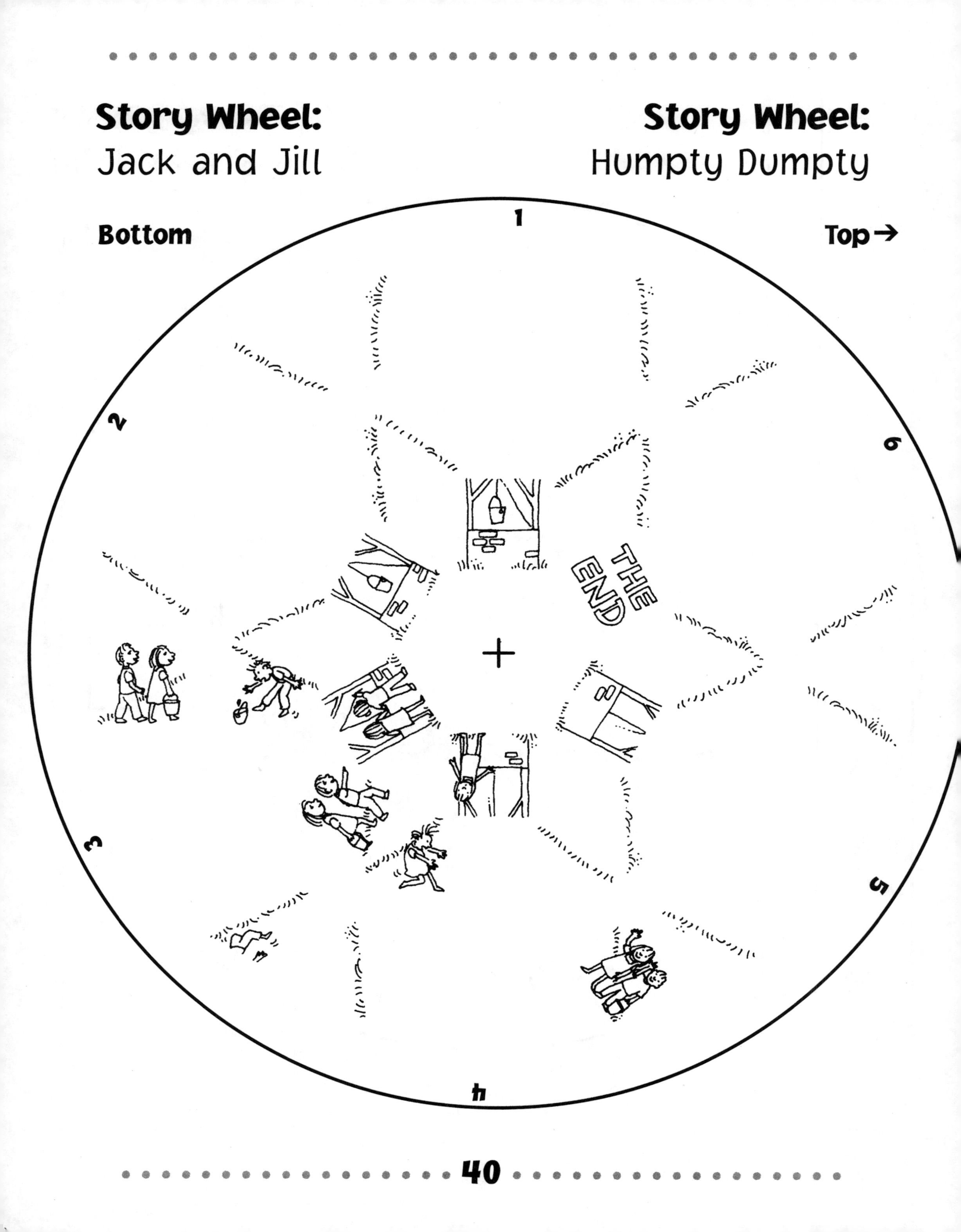
Story Wheel:
Jack and Jill
Story Wheel:
Humpty Dumpty
Bottom
Top→
1
2
3
4
5
6
THE END
40

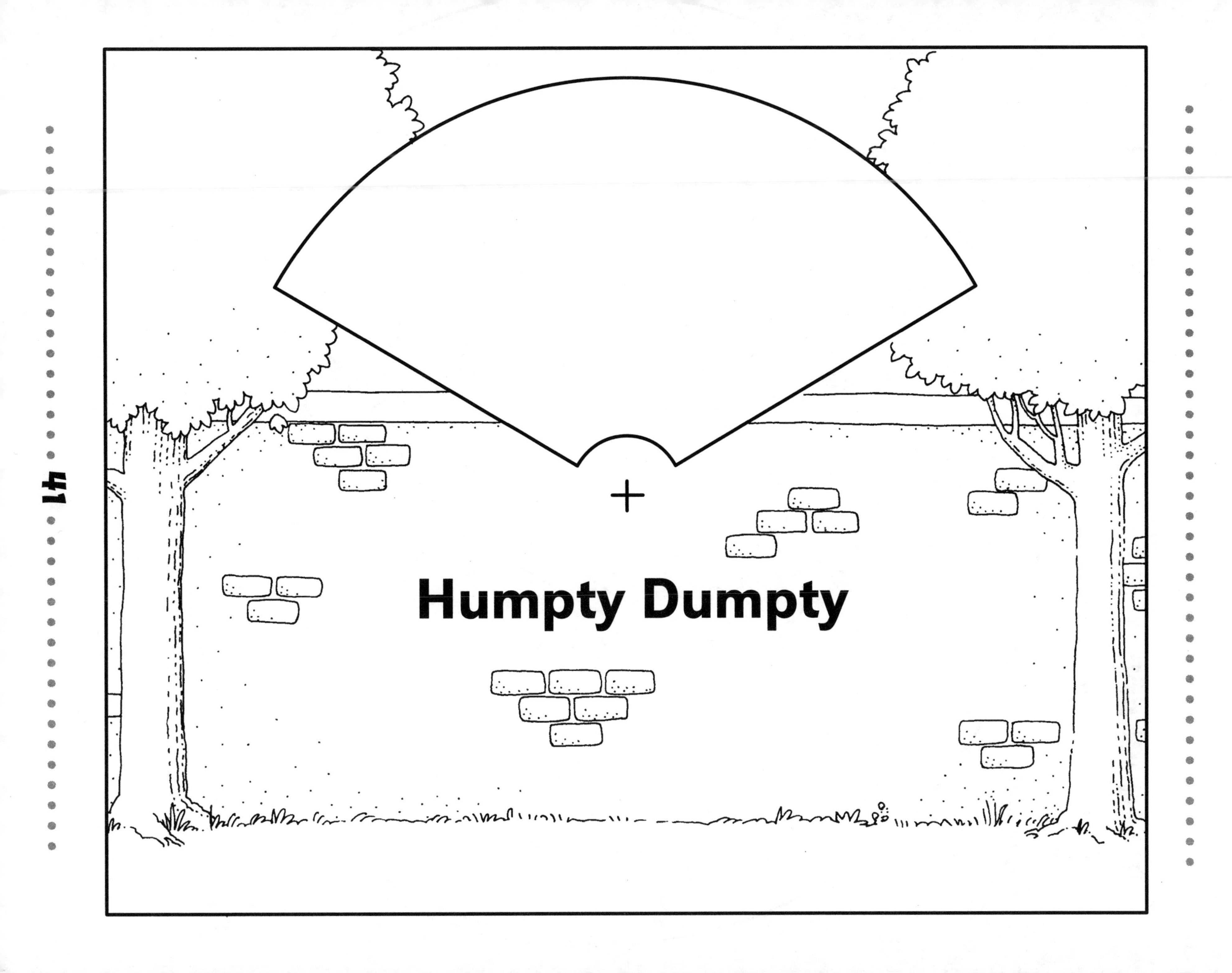
Humpty Dumpty

Story Wheel: Humpty Dumpty

Bottom

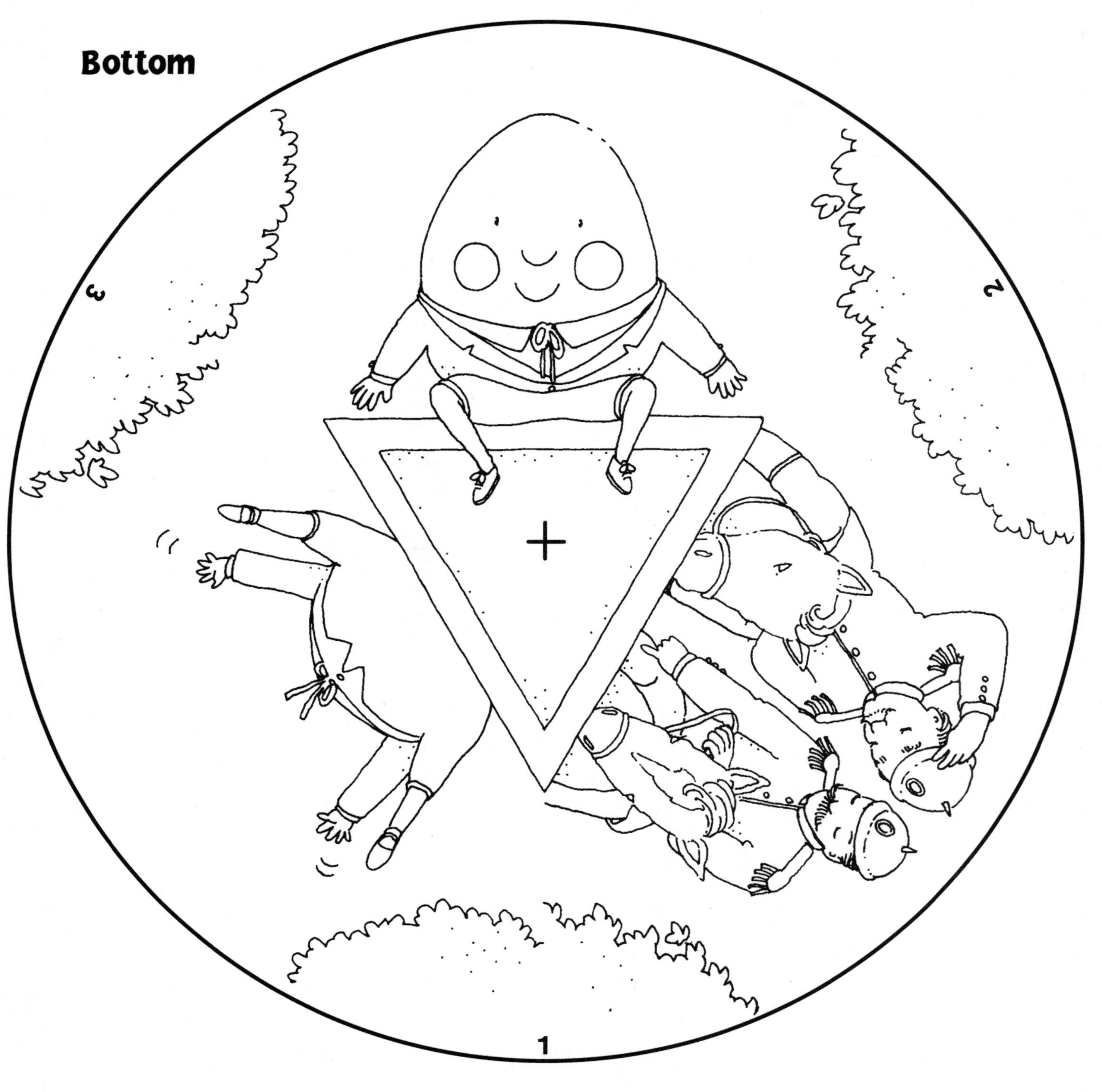

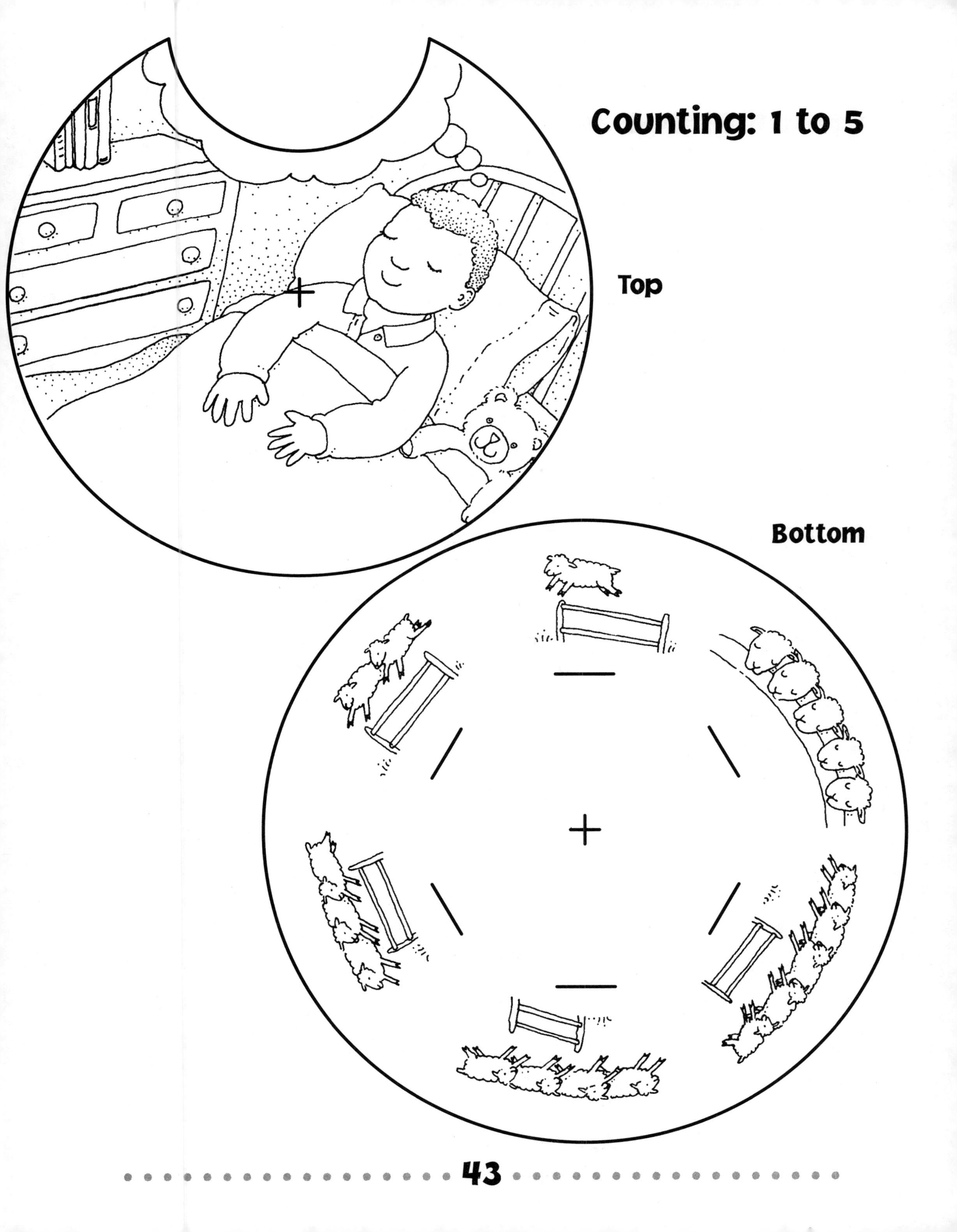
Counting: 1 to 5
Top
Bottom

Counting: 6 to 10

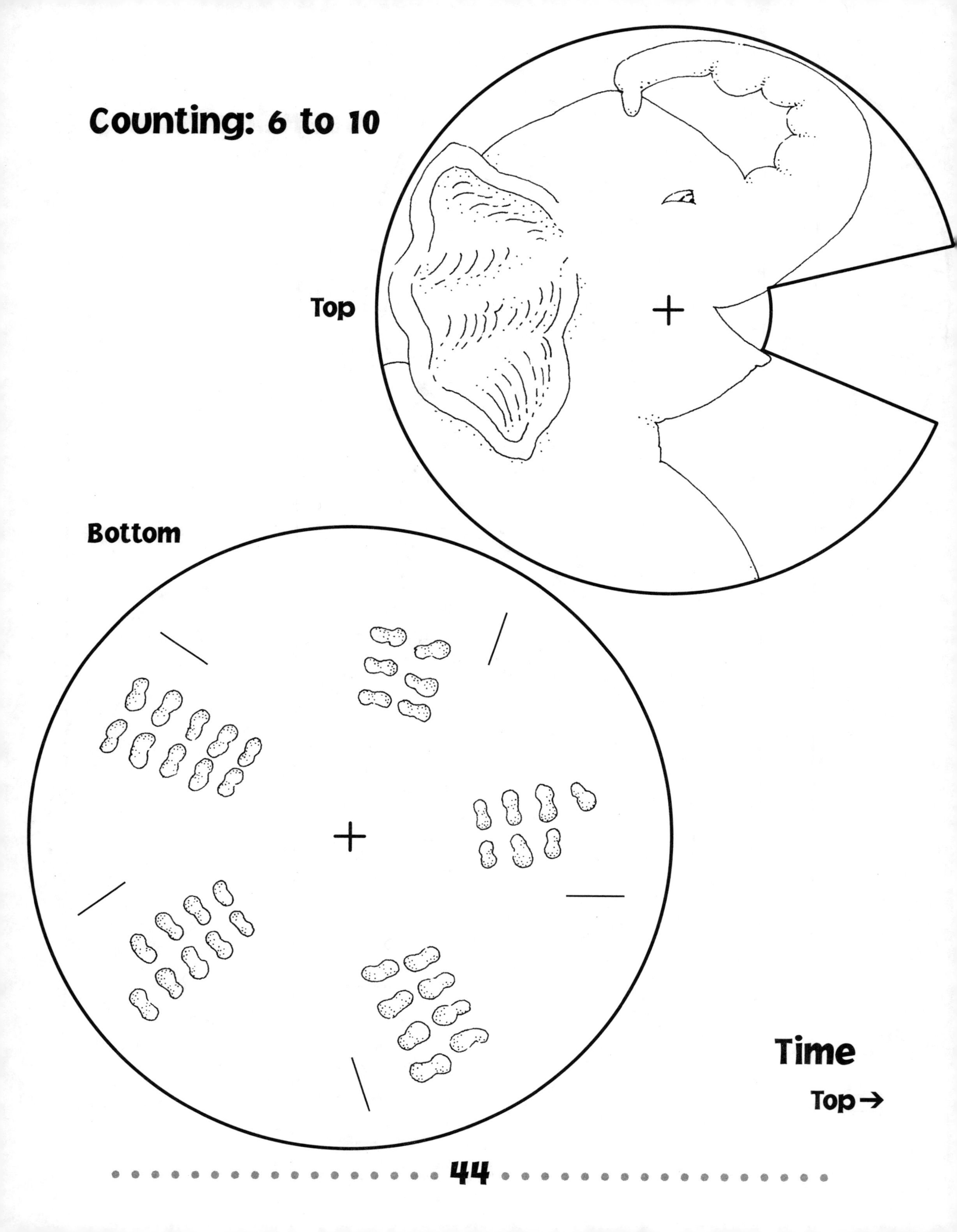

Bottom

Top→

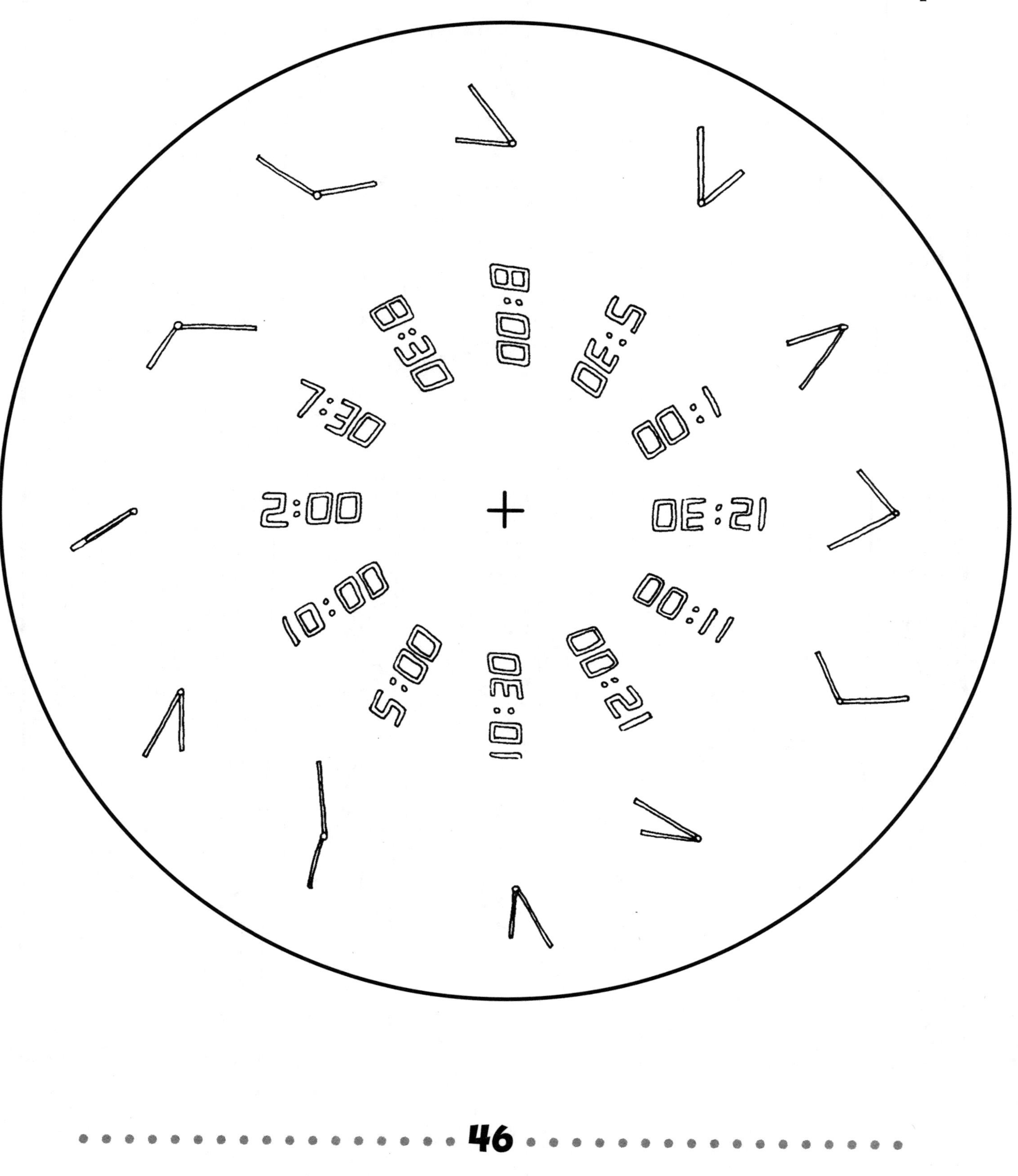

Number Facts

Bottom

More Number Facts

Top→

+

More Number Facts

Bottom

Money

Top→

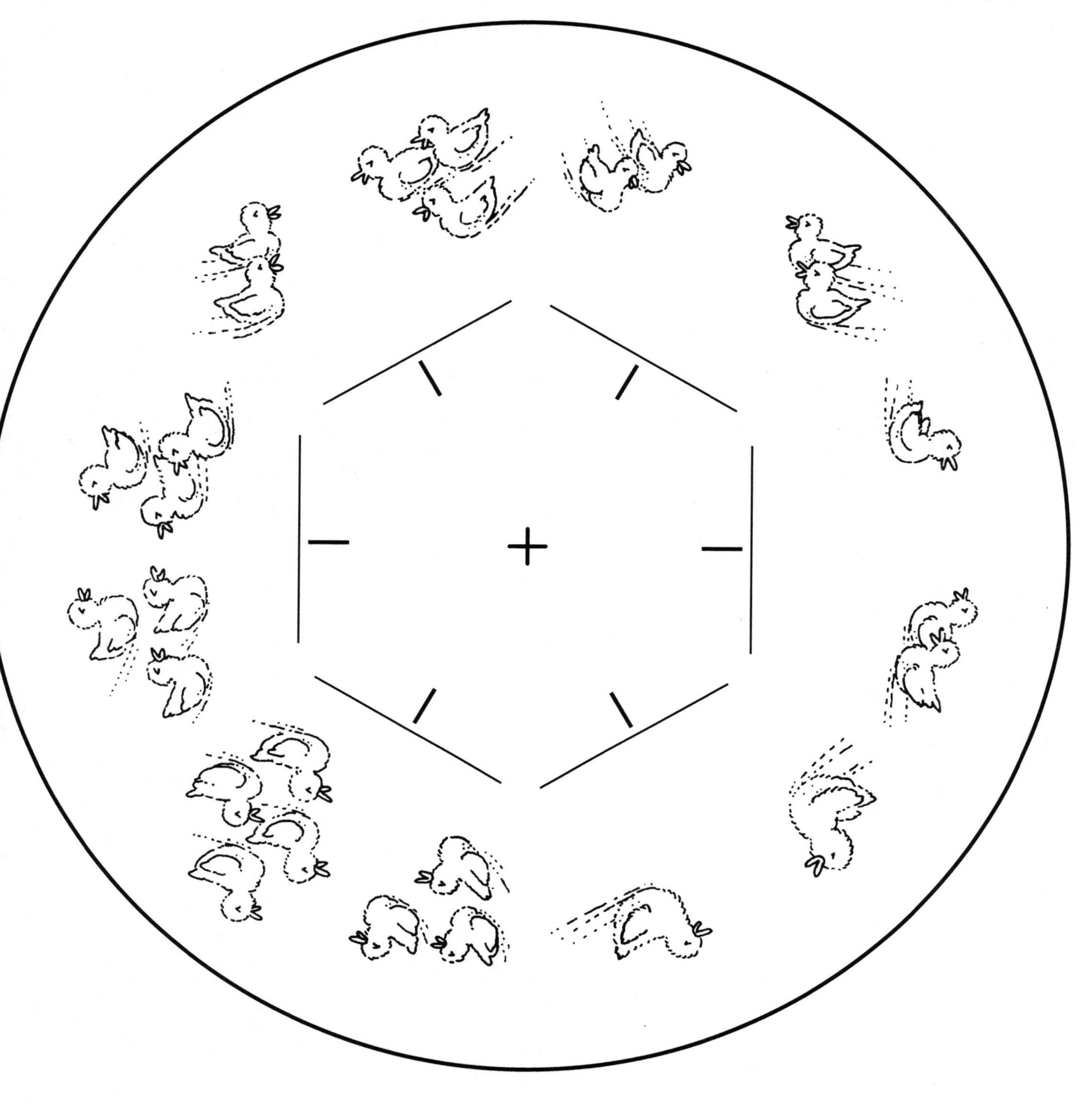

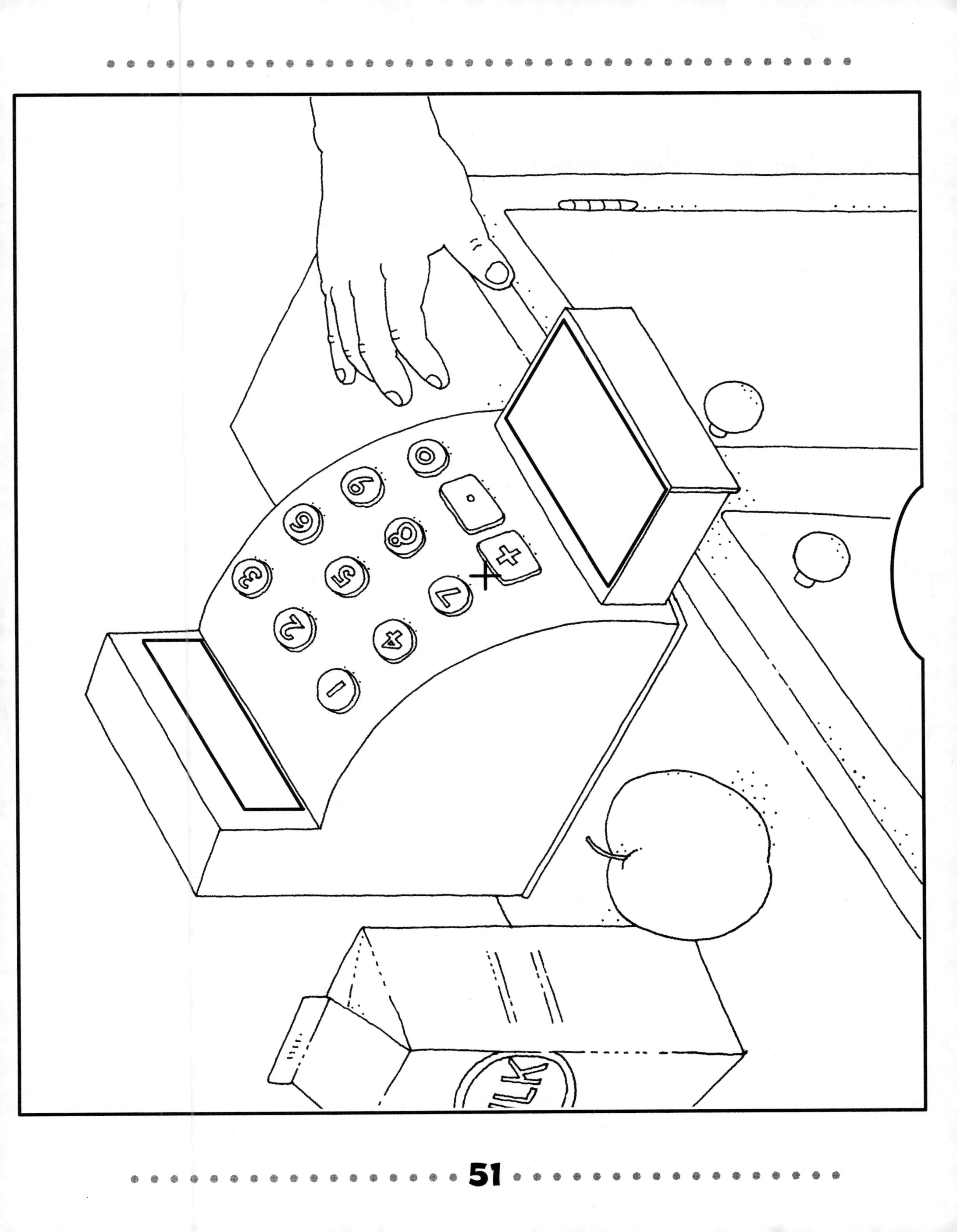

Money

Bottom

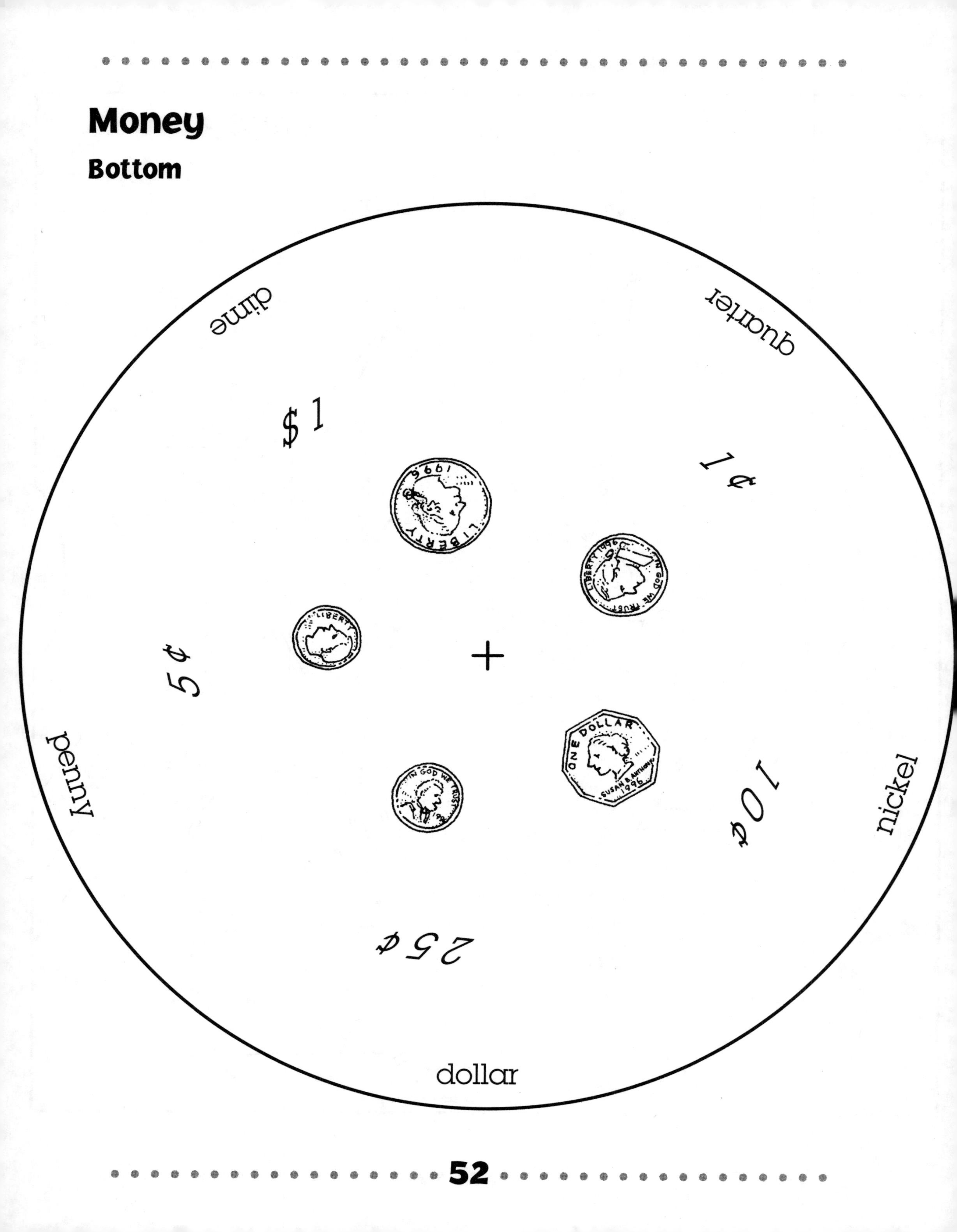

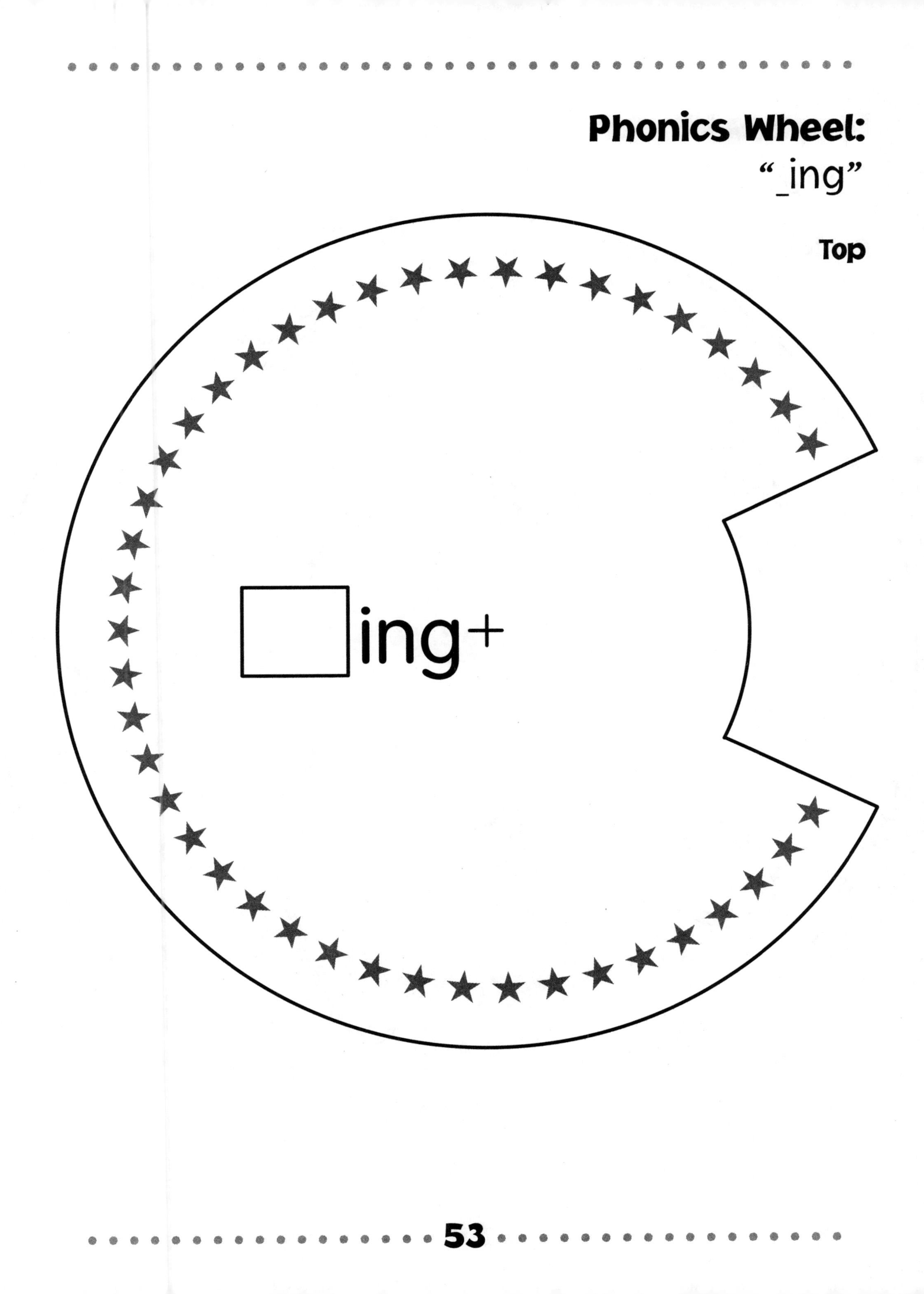
Phonics Wheel:
"_ing"
Top
ing+

Phonics Wheel:
“_ing”

Bottom

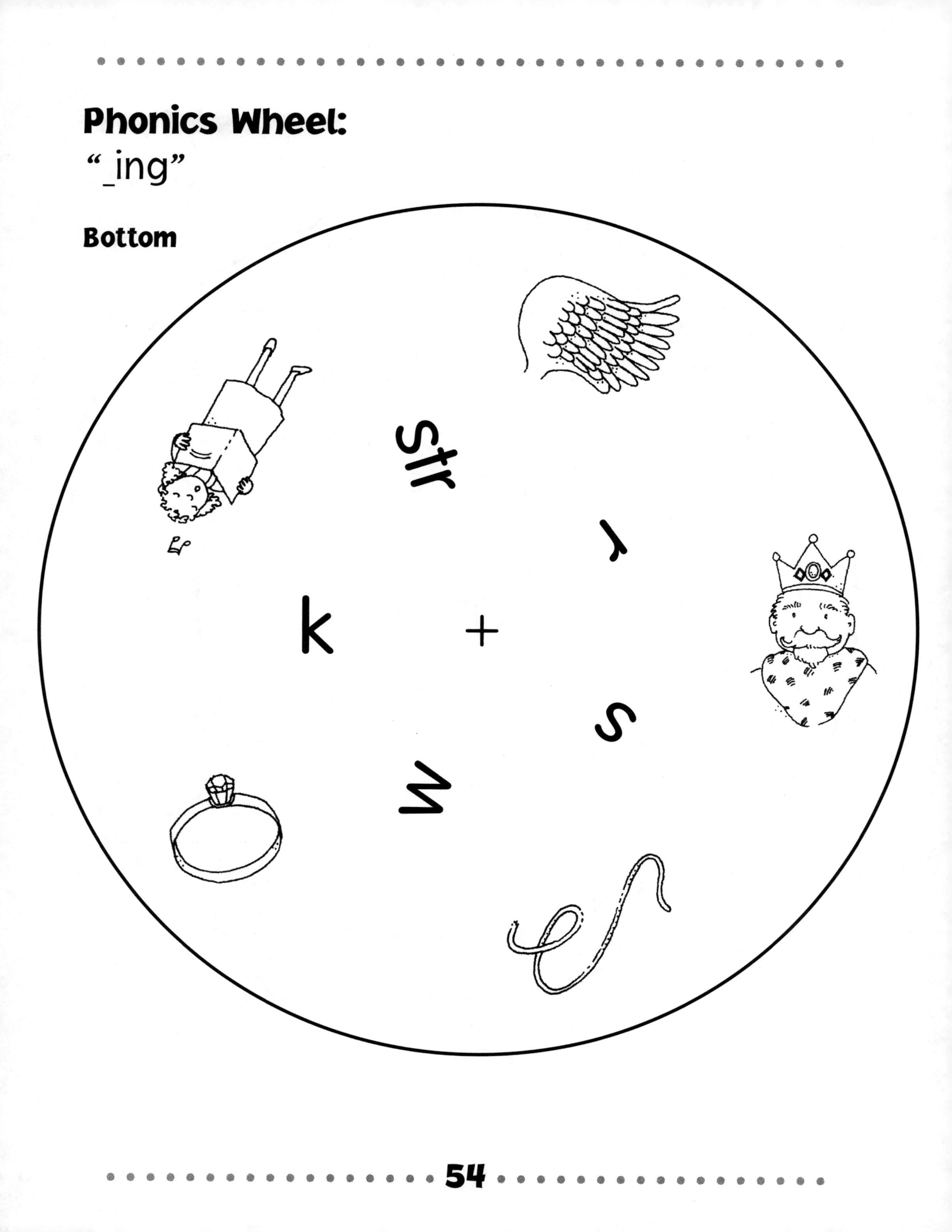

Phonics Wheel:

“_ook”

Top

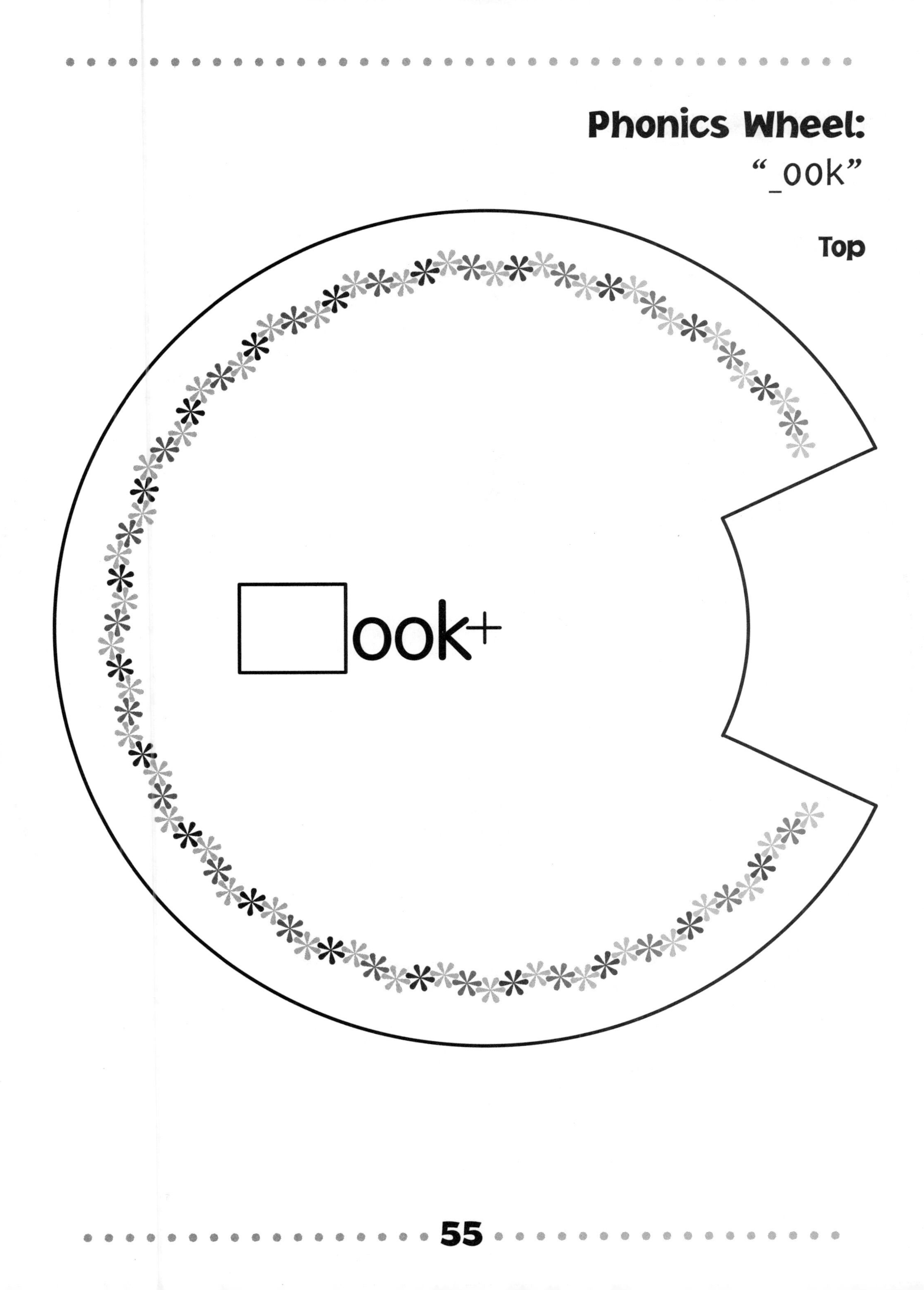

Phonics Wheel:
"_ook"

Bottom

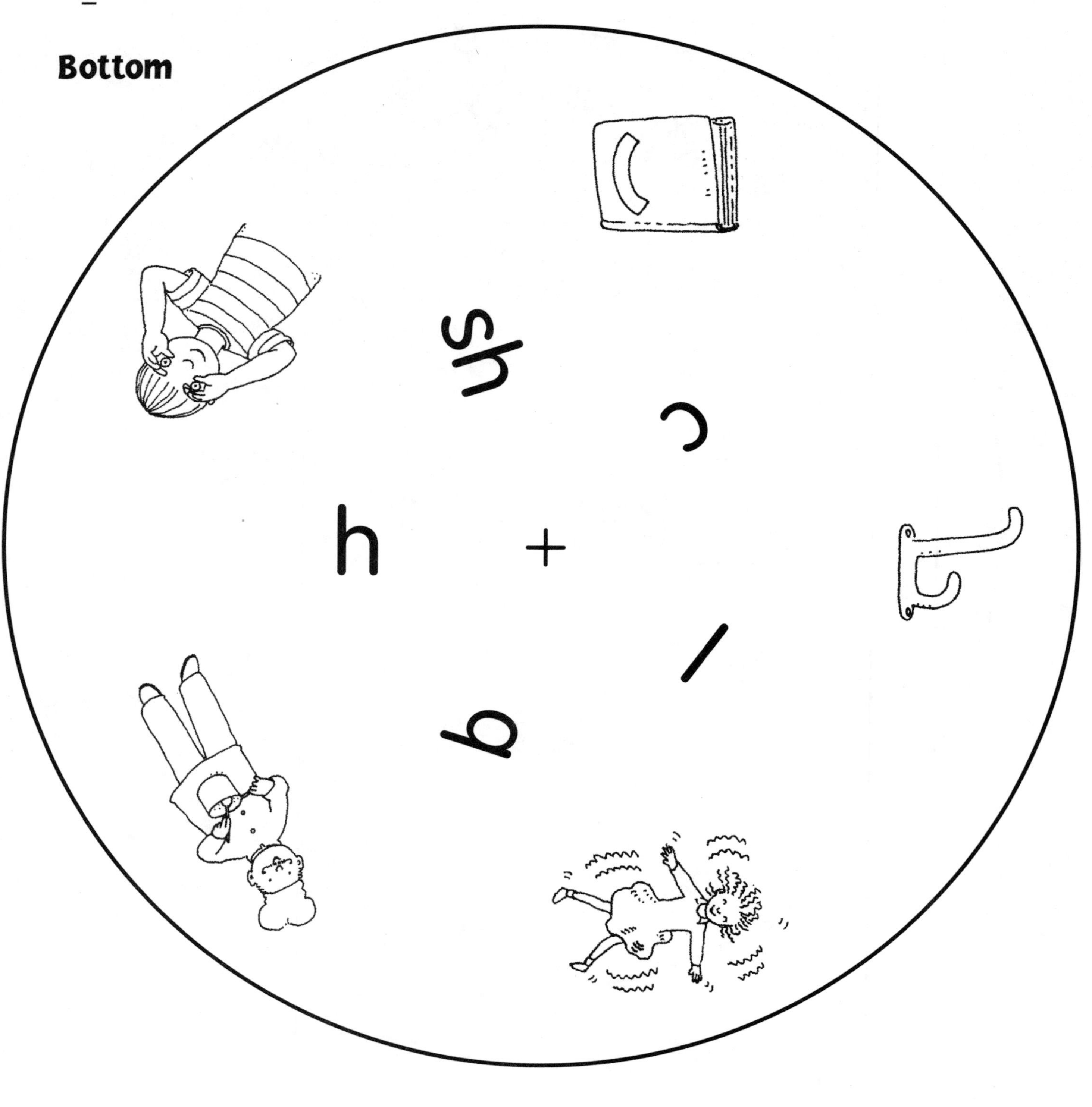

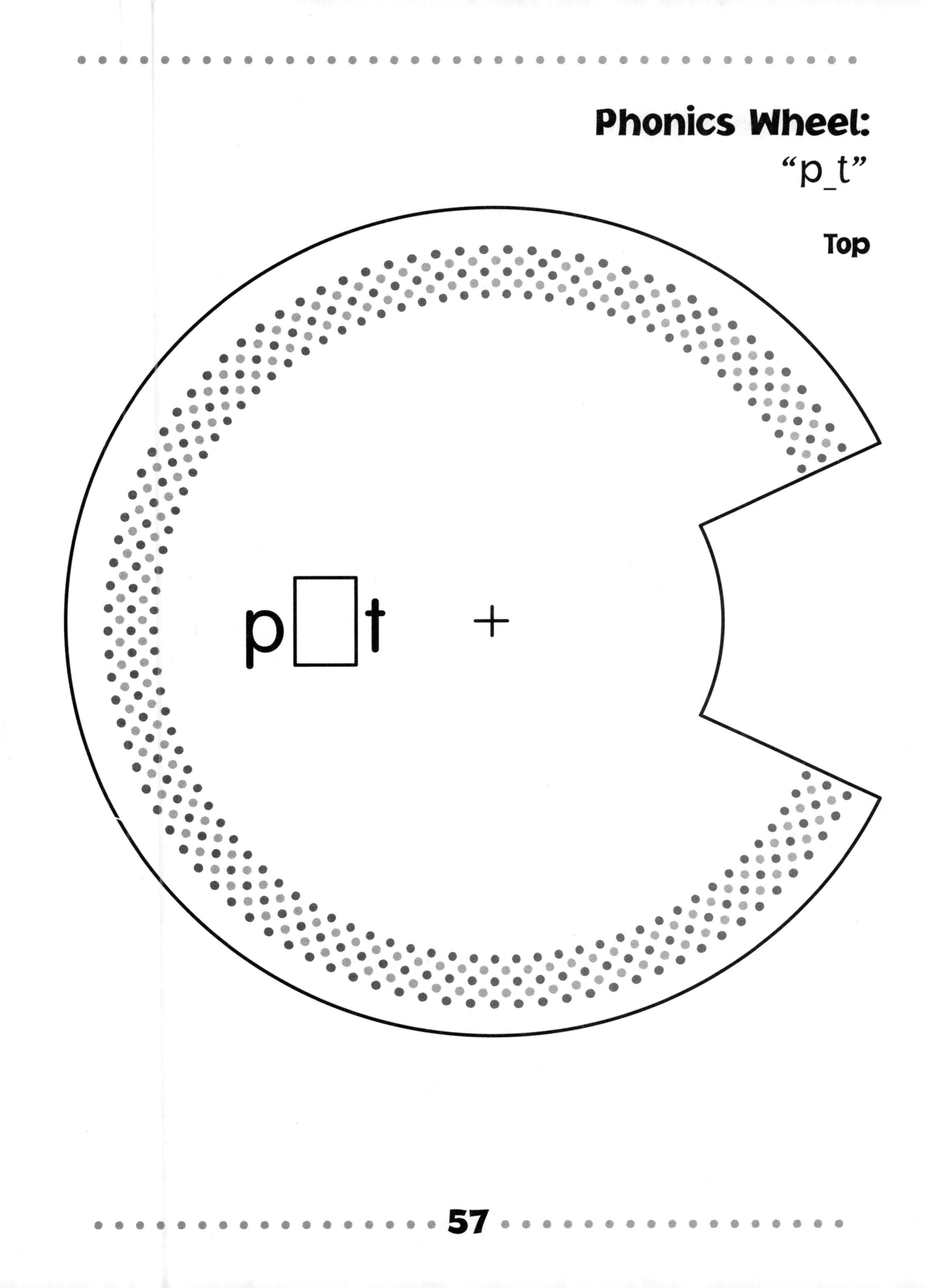
Phonics Wheel:
“p_t”
Top
p t

Phonics Wheel:
"p_t"

Bottom

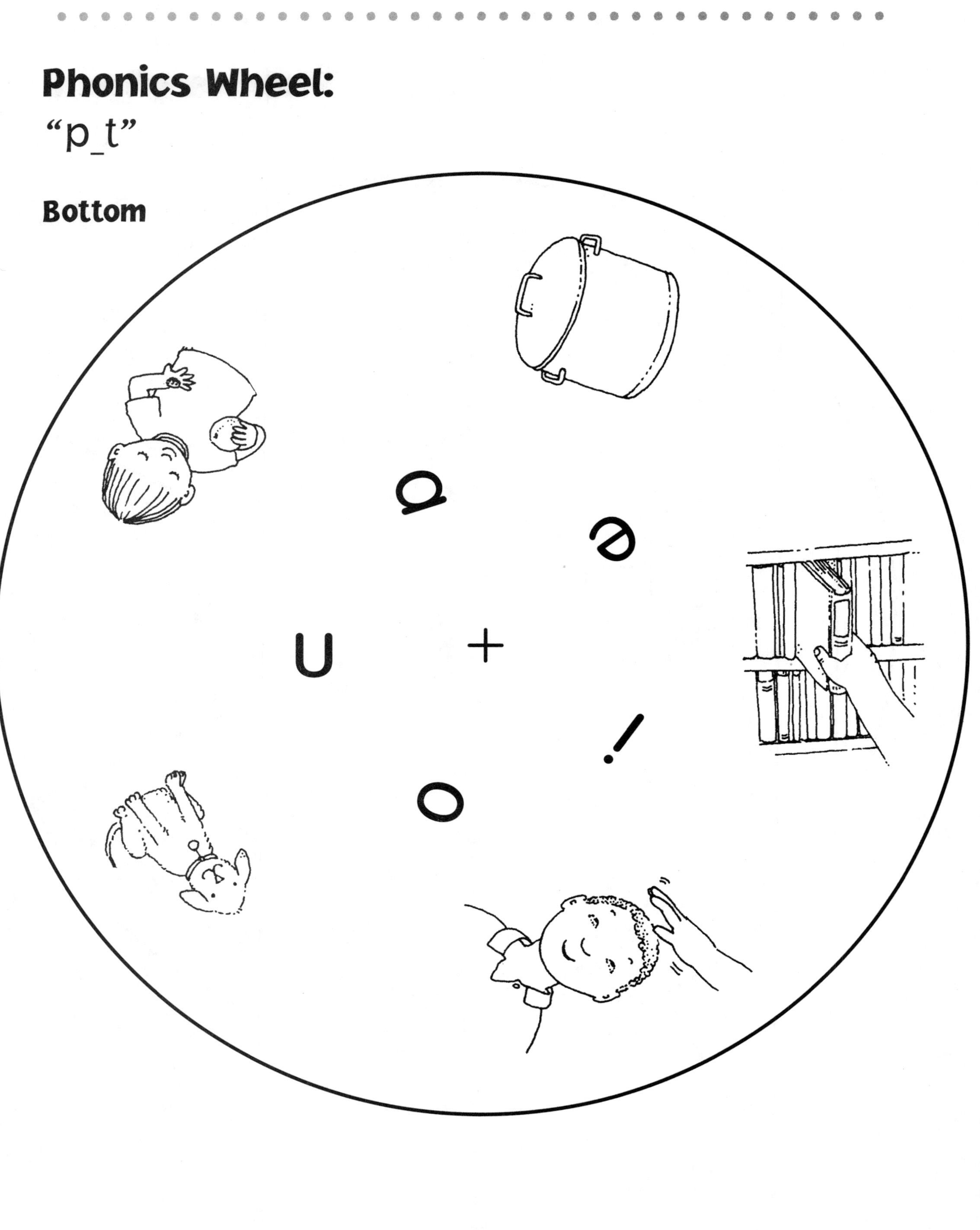

Phonics Wheel:

"sh_"

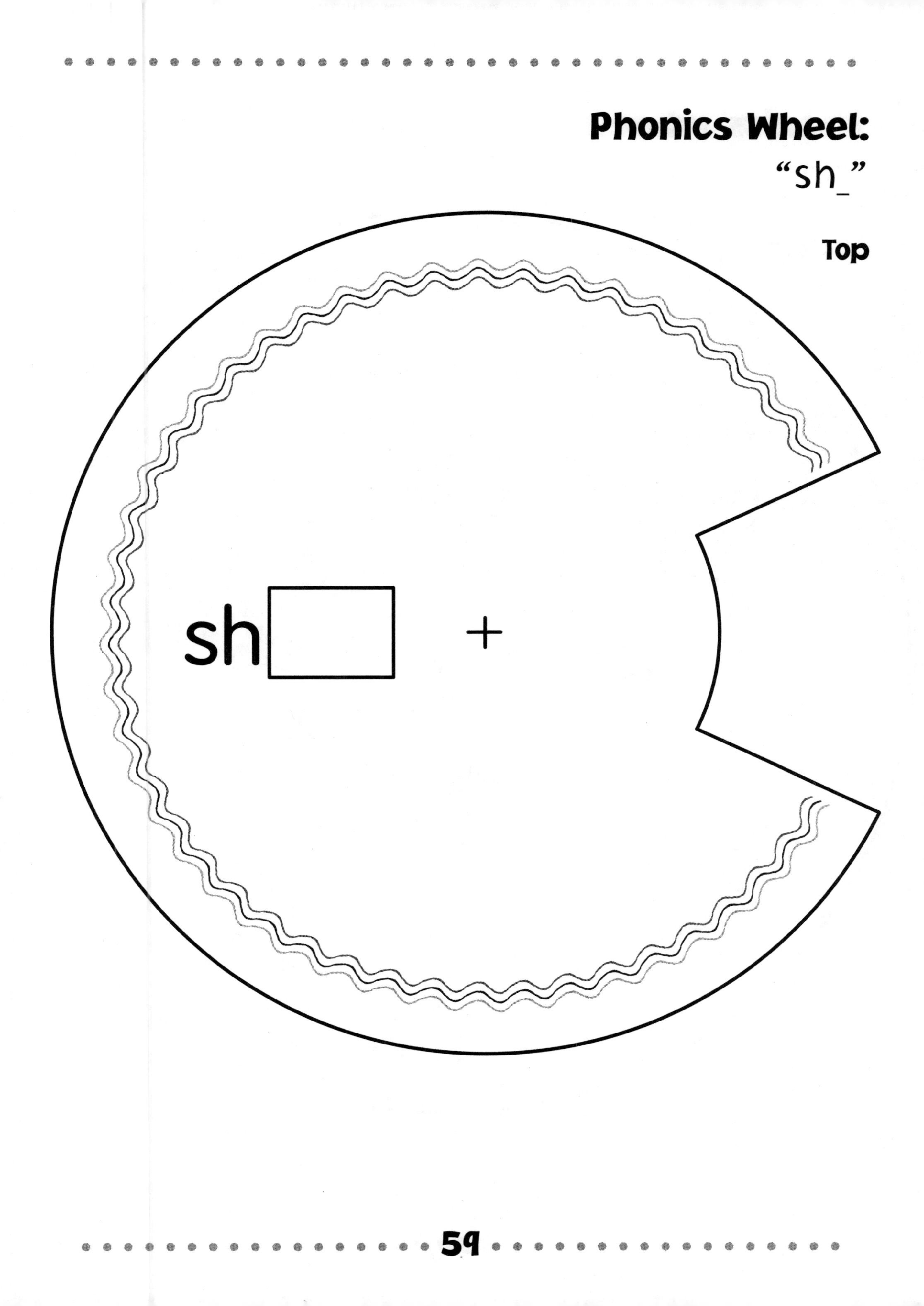

Phonics Wheel:
"sh_"

Bottom

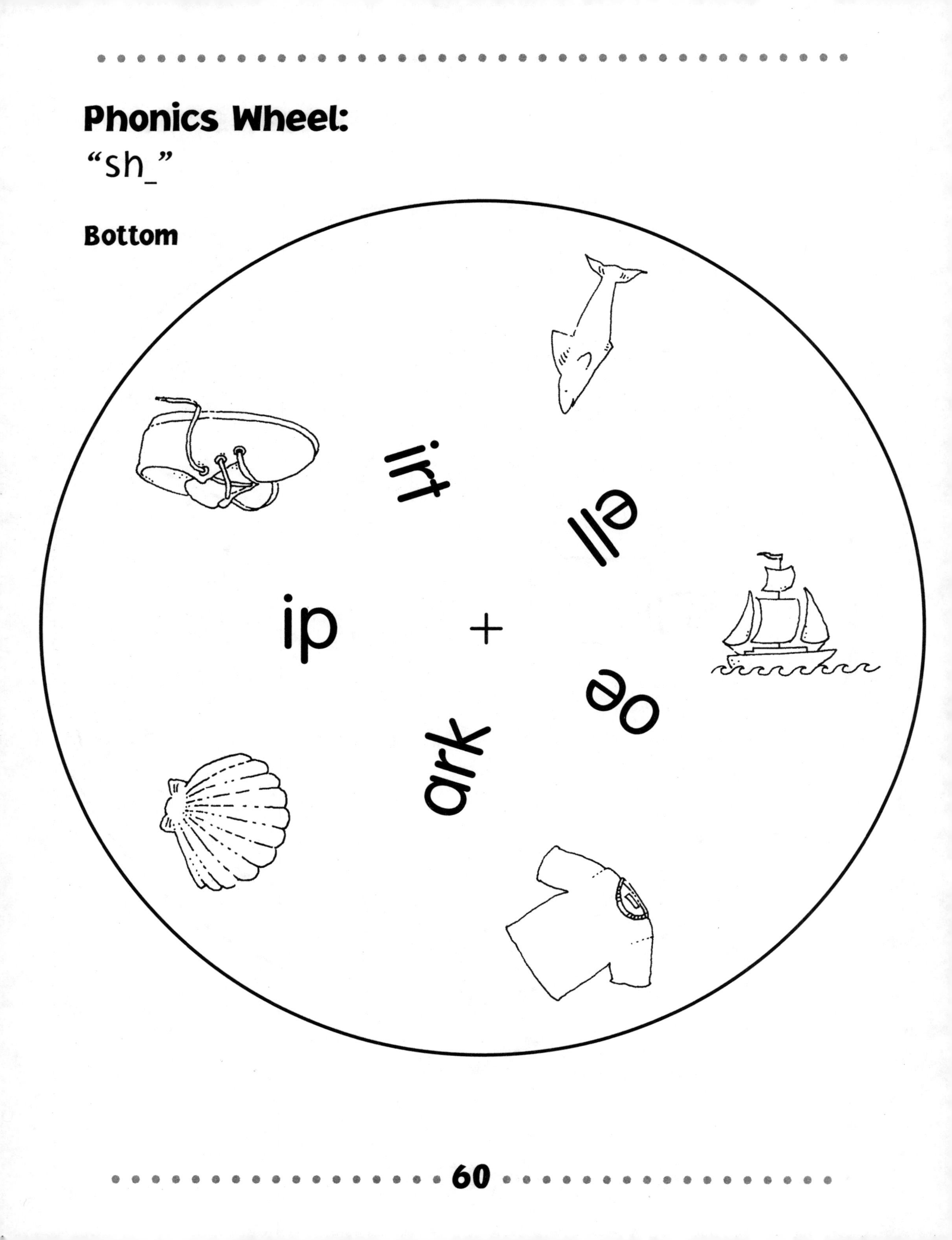

Blank Story Wheel

Top

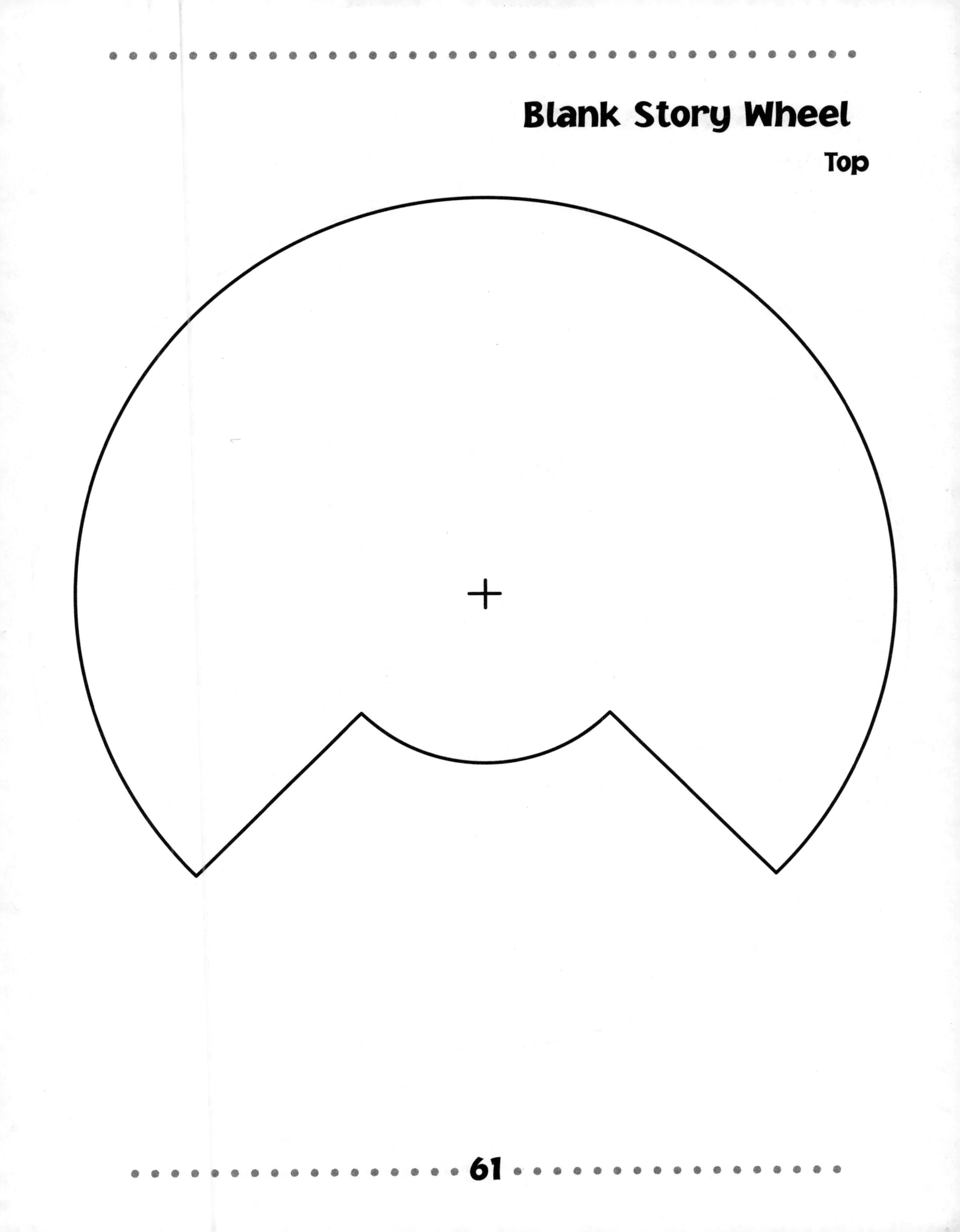

Blank Story Wheel

Bottom

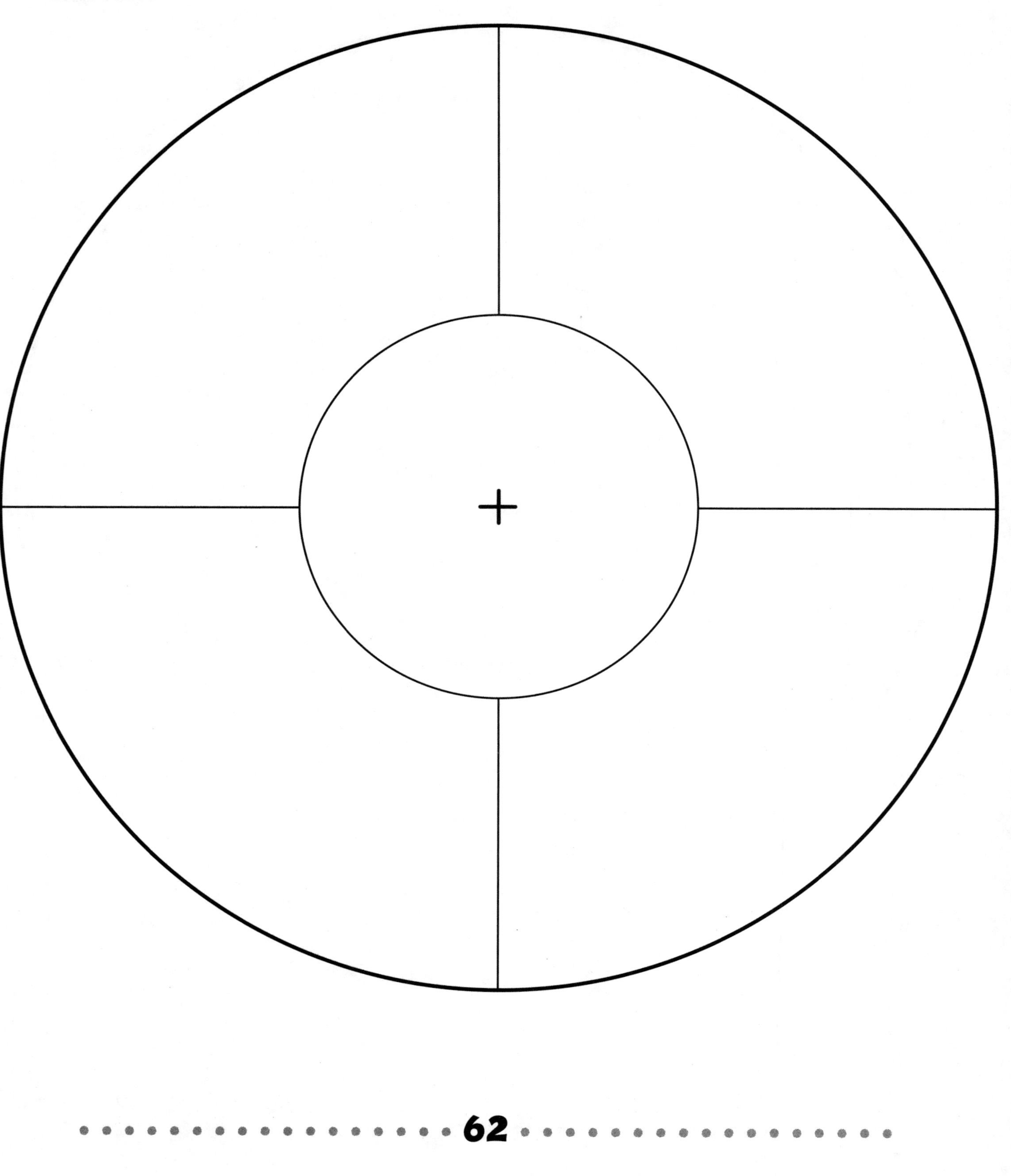

Blank Word Wheel

Top

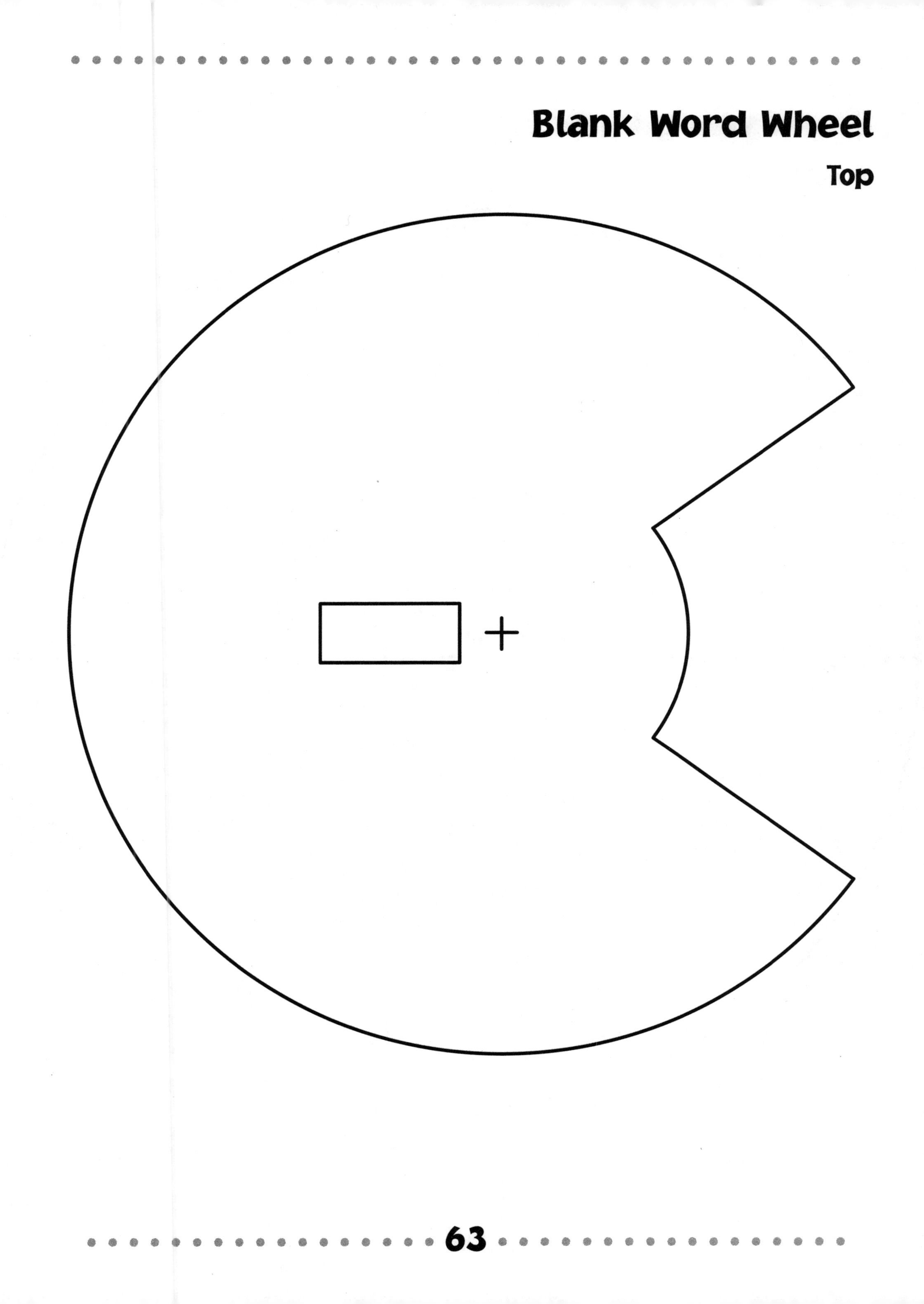

Blank Word Wheel

Bottom

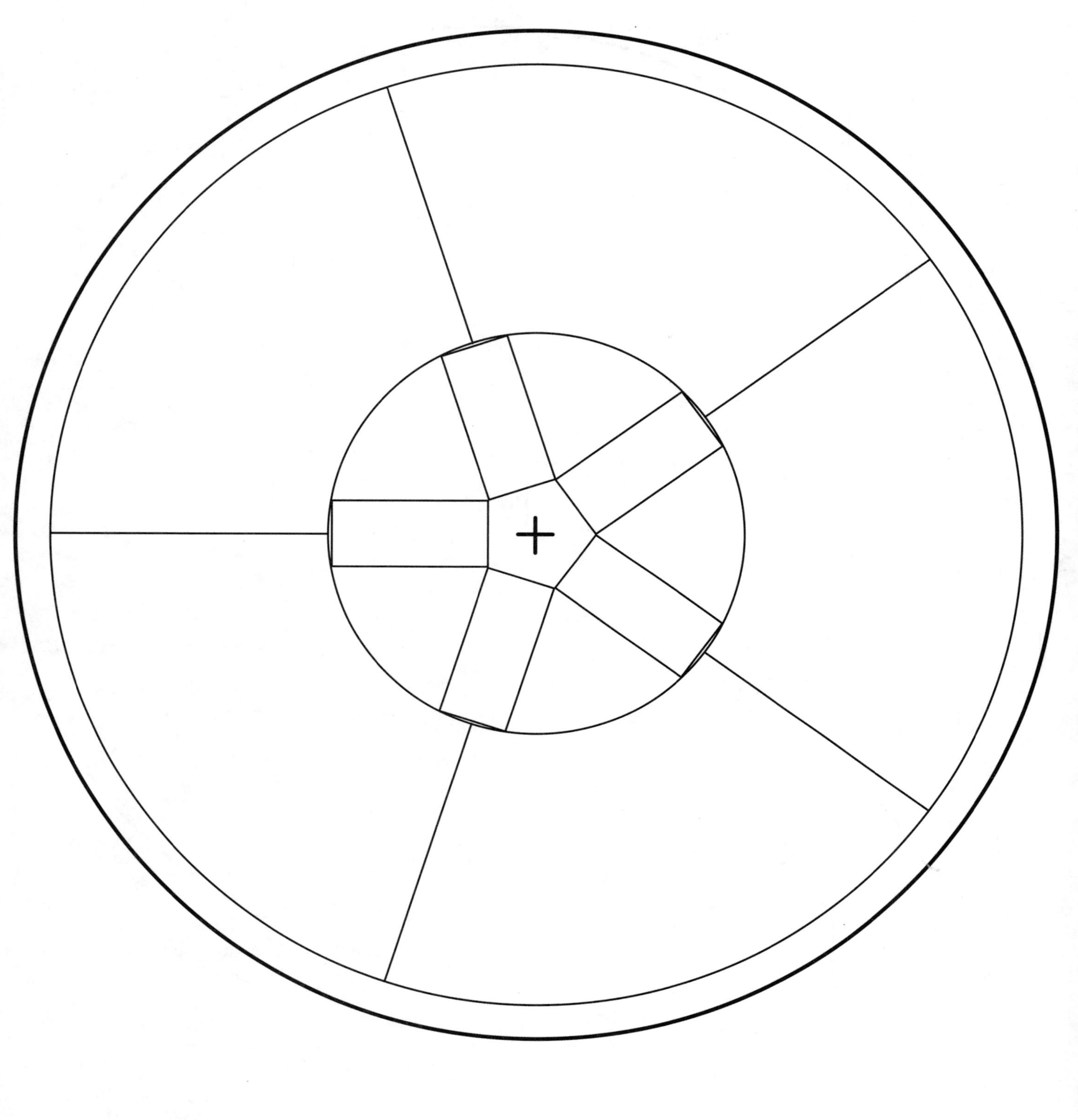